"You, I'm afraid, are just plain wrong."

Jayne turned her back to Chris and reached for the doorknob. "Now that we've got that settled, I think the best place for you to sleep is—"

"The hell we have." Chris strode forward, grabbed her forearm and pulled her around to face him while shutting the door with a single kick. Then he gripped her other elbow. "I learned every inch of your body when we were seventeen."

She stopped struggling and stared at him, mouth open.

He nodded. "You have a birthmark on your left hip, red and shaped like a boot." Her gasp made him smile. "Oh, yeah, I've seen it. I've kissed it. Want to tell me now that I'm plain wrong?"

Before his next heartbeat, the lights went out.

Dear Reader,

Though my family moved to Florida when I was nine, I still treasure Christmas memories from my early years in the Smoky Mountains. I recall sitting on the curb of a downtown street, waiting for Santa to arrive at the end of the Christmas parade. I remember watching red and green traffic signals blinking like ornaments in the falling snow.

Of course, I remember opening presents in front of the tree on Christmas mornings. Then we'd dress in our holiday best and drive to my grandmother's house, where my cousins and aunts and uncles would all gather for a splendid Christmas dinner.

Sometimes, though, Christmas doesn't turn out as you expect. A natural disaster—say, a blizzard—can make travel impossible, keeping you from the ones you love or, worse, shutting you in with someone you don't trust. The electric power might fail. How will you stay warm? What will you eat? Will rescue arrive soon enough?

These challenges confront Jayne Thomas when she's marooned over the winter holidays with some of her students at the Hawkridge School. The unexpected arrival of sexy photojournalist Chris Hammond eases the burden of looking after the girls, but his disturbing presence threatens Jayne's emotional balance. Chris says he knows her, insists they have a past together. Jayne doesn't remember him at all. Which one of them is telling the truth?

I hope you enjoy spending time in the snowy wonderland of the Smoky Mountains. I love to hear from readers at any time of the year, so feel free to write me at P.O. Box 1012, Vass, NC 28389.

Happy holidays!

Lynnette Kent

A Holiday
to Remember
LYNNETTE KENT

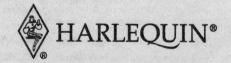

HARLEQUIN®

TORONTO • NEW YORK • LONDON
AMSTERDAM • PARIS • SYDNEY • HAMBURG
STOCKHOLM • ATHENS • TOKYO • MILAN • MADRID
PRAGUE • WARSAW • BUDAPEST • AUCKLAND

Recycling programs
for this product may
not exist in your area.

ISBN-13: 978-0-373-75288-1

A HOLIDAY TO REMEMBER

ABOUT THE AUTHOR

Lynnette Kent began writing her first romance in the fourth grade, about a ship's stowaway who would fall in love with her captain, Christopher Columbus. Years of scribbling later, her husband suggested she write one of those "Harlequin romances" she loved to read. With his patience and the support of her two daughters, Lynnette realized her dream of being a published novelist. She now lives in North Carolina, where she divides her time between books—writing and reading—and the horses she adores. Feel free to contact Lynnette via her Web site, www.lynnette-kent.com.

Books by Lynnette Kent

This book is dedicated to all the wonderful workers at Harlequin Books who type and copy and proofread pages, who design and illustrate covers, who run the machines that put pages together, who fill and ship boxes and perform countless other tasks I'm not even aware of…in other words, the people who see to it that my stories get into print. Thank you!

Chapter One

Chris Hammond had never thought of himself as a stalker.

But he needed to get another look at the face of the woman who'd entered the coffee shop just as he was leaving. They'd danced together on the threshold for a few seconds, trying to get out of each other's way. He'd backed up, finally, and held the door open for her. With a quick smile and a "Happy Holidays," she'd headed inside as Chris stepped out onto the sidewalk.

Now he turned toward the wide front window to find her again. The service counter ran across the back of the room, so all he could see of his quarry was an auburn ponytail fanned over the back of a heavy gray coat appropriate for the subfreezing mountain weather.

Maybe the hair had triggered his memory. A long time ago he'd known a girl with a mane in that same polished mahogany color, with the same extravagant curls. He'd been a kid then, but coming back to Ridgeville, North Carolina, had brought those days closer to the surface.

That's why he hadn't been here in over a decade.

Chris didn't think the hair was the only resemblance, though. Something about her face had seemed familiar enough to stop his heartbeat for a second or two. He wanted to be sure he was wrong about recognizing those hazel eyes, the lightly freckled cheeks and pointed chin. Then he could finish grocery shopping for his granddad with a clear head.

So he lingered in front of the adjacent hardware store next to the coffee shop, waiting for the woman and hoping like hell she wasn't meeting a gaggle of friends for an hour's gossip over coffee. He'd have frozen to death by then, despite his new down-filled jacket. His last assignment, in equatorial Africa, had left him with a poor tolerance for cold.

Every time the bell on the shop door tinkled, he glanced that way from beneath the lowered brim of his baseball cap. Six times he was disappointed, but seven had always been his lucky number and proved so yet again—he saw the gray sleeve of her coat as she pushed the door open.

He tipped his hat back, wanting to get a good look as she approached. The coffee place was the last business at this end of Main Street. Surely she would come his way.

Instead, the woman walked straight to the curb, showing him only her profile. She checked both ways for traffic before stepping into the street, but he missed seeing her full face because that one glimpse of her tip-tilted nose and full lower lip had left him gasping for air, like he'd been sucker punched.

Such a likeness couldn't be an accident. What the hell was going on?

Using instincts refined by ten years spent in war zones around the world, Chris followed her. Chaos had replaced logic in his brain. He knew only two things. One—dead people did not come back to life. He'd seen enough of them to be absolutely certain of that. So she couldn't be the person he thought she was. But just in case...

Two—he wouldn't get a decent night's sleep until he made damn sure he'd never met this woman before.

WITH EVERY PASSING MINUTE, Jayne Thomas became more convinced. And concerned.

She was being stalked.

She'd noticed him first at Beautiful Beans, when she was going in as he came out. Well, what woman wouldn't notice him? Big, but not in the least fat, graceful yet at the same time unquestionably male, with piercing blue eyes·and light brown hair curling at his temples and the nape of his neck. A respectable stubble of beard shadowed his square chin and sensual mouth. The man was, in the vernacular of her students, seriously hot.

Headmistresses of private schools did not deal in seriously hot men, however, so she'd resisted the impulse to invite him back into the shop for more coffee. Anyway, she had errands to run. She'd just wanted to warm up first.

As she waited her turn to order, though, she'd felt an itching between her shoulder blades. A backward glance had shown her the same man, now standing on the sidewalk, staring inside from underneath the brim of a Yankees baseball cap.

Surely not at her, though. She wasn't the type to draw attention from a man who could take his pick of the beautiful women in any room he entered. Especially here in Ridgeville, Jayne noted, as one of the young women seated at a table sent him a wink through the window, then pouted when he didn't notice.

Leaving the coffee shop, Jayne saw the man again, in front of Gibbs's Hardware. Waiting to take advantage of that flirtatious wink, after all?

No, because he followed *her* across the street and into Woolgathering. He did not look like the knitting type, but he appeared fascinated by the different wools along every aisle she visited. Though he never addressed her directly, time and time again Jayne felt the burn of his gaze.

Finally, she ducked into the back corner and cowered

behind the mohair display, hoping to wait him out. As a result, she spent too much on needles and wool for a sweater she wouldn't have time to work on over the school's winter break. At least he'd left when she emerged.

He turned up again in Miller's Candy Kitchen about five minutes after she walked in. A coincidence, maybe, since the yarn shop was right next door. Then Jayne recrossed Main Street and stepped into Angela's Art Supplies and Gallery. The blue-eyed stranger appeared in the wide front window only seconds later, apparently consumed with interest in a papier-mâché crèche from Italy.

"He's waiting for me to come out," Jayne told Angela, as they pretended to examine the art pencils. "What am I going to do?"

"Leave by the back door," Angela suggested, in her precise English accent. "Give him the slip, so to speak."

She nodded. "Of course." She squeezed Angela's elbow with gratitude and made her getaway, hurrying along the alley behind the string of businesses to her real destination, Kringle's Toy Store.

Sitting at his desk in the back room, Mr. Kringle looked up from his account books as she slipped in the rear entrance. "A welcome, if unconventional, arrival," he said. "What can I do for you today, Miss Thomas?"

"I have five students staying at school over the break, and I want to have some new, enjoyable activities to keep them occupied."

"Of course." His German accent and courtly manner soothed her agitation. "I have just what you're searching for." He led the way to a shelf filled with bright holiday-themed boxes.

"These are the finest crackers I could order." He picked up a box with a cellophane window that showed one of the paper-

and-cardboard containers called "crackers" in England. "Each contains a selection of candies and a variety of prizes— jewelry, games and so forth." He made a motion with his hands, as if pulling on the two ends of the cracker. "And a delicious pop! when they are opened." He leaned closer to whisper, "I tried one myself."

"They're lovely. But…" Jayne shook her head. "We don't make a fuss over the holidays. The girls tend to get homesick, even if they chose to stay at school, and celebrating makes them feel worse. I'll just look around for a while. We'll need games to fill the time, maybe some paint-by-number kits and puzzles. I want to keep them too busy to mope."

Mr. Kringle smoothed his long brown mustache. "It's a good thing you do. These girls are lucky they have you to care for them."

Jayne smiled at him, then spent an hour choosing diversions for her winter break boarders. As headmistress of the Hawkridge School, and with no family of her own, she stayed over the vacations with those students who would not be going home. Hawkridge provided a last resort for teenagers with emotional problems that threatened to ruin the rest of their lives through drug addiction, alcoholism, risky sexual involvements and other dangerous behaviors. Given the temptations offered by the holiday season, some parents couldn't face the prospect of coping with challenges not yet resolved. Less often, a girl would rather remain at school than return to an abusive or uncomfortable home.

Without exception, however, these troubled girls needed the haven. Hawkridge had never had a student fail to come back from the winter break.

With her purchases stowed in two heavy shopping bags, Jayne wished Mr. Kringle a Happy Hanukkah in response to his

"Merry Christmas" as he opened the front door for her. Pausing in the sheltered entryway, she shifted one of the bags to her left hand, then turned to head up the sidewalk toward her car.

"Took you long enough."

Jayne gasped and jerked her head up. The stalker stood in front of her, blocking her way. She'd put him out of her mind in the cheery atmosphere of the toy shop. Now he loomed over her, seeming bigger than before, definitely more threatening. He wasn't smiling.

"Got a lot of kids to buy presents for, I guess?" His smooth, deep voice held an undercurrent of anger.

Chills shuddered down her spine, spreading fear to the tips of her fingers and the soles of her feet. The wind felt colder than it had earlier this morning. Main Street seemed more deserted.

But when she glanced around, Jayne saw that she erred in her impression of emptiness. There were still plenty of people going in and out of the stores nearby. No one could hurt her with all these folks watching.

The knowledge stiffened her shoulders and lifted her chin. "Yes, I do. Why are you following me?"

Instead of answering, he stared at her face. Jayne glared back at him while tightening her grip on the shopping bags. They were heavy enough to serve as weapons if she needed them.

"Jayne Thomas," he said, finally. "You say that's your name?"

"Yes. Why are you following me?"

He shook his head once, as if clearing a fly away. "Are you from Ridgeville?"

Her fear was giving way to irritation. "I don't owe you any information whatsoever. Certainly not until you identify yourself and what you want. Why are you following me?" She raised her voice this time, hoping to get the attention of someone nearby.

The man grabbed her upper arm and jerked her toward him. "Have you always lived here?" The set of his jaw hinted at violence.

Her heart pounded. "I—"

"Trouble, Miz Thomas?" Steve Greeley, one of the county's deputy sheriffs, came up beside her. "What's going on?"

The grip on her arm fell away. "Nothing," the stranger said. "I thought Miss Thomas was an old friend."

Jayne gazed at him through narrowed eyes. "You were wrong. I've never seen you before in my life."

After a moment, one side of his mouth twitched into a half smile. His gaze, however, remained steely. "Sorry. You look just like…well, somebody else." He glanced at Deputy Greeley. "I'm Chris Hammond, Charlie Hammond's grandson. I'll be staying with him for a few days. That's my bike on the other side of the street. You can watch me out of sight."

"I'll do that," Greeley promised.

Jayne, too, observed as Chris Hammond crossed Main Street and walked down the hill to a huge motorcycle parked at the curb. Black and chrome, the bike seemed to take up as much space as her own Jeep. The roar, as he fired the engine, rolled through her like an earthquake.

The noise died away once the bike topped the hill and headed down the other side. Steve turned to Jayne. "Are you sure you're okay?"

"I'm just fine. He worried me a little, following me around town. But if I looked like someone he knew, I guess that makes sense." She hunched her shoulders and relaxed them again. "I'd better get these bags to the car. My arms are starting to stretch."

"Here, let me." The deputy took the bags, walked with her to the Jeep and stowed them in the backseat. "Do you have anywhere else you need to shop, Jayne? I could go with you, in case that weirdo comes back."

"No, thanks. I've got to head back to the school. Tonight is our official end of term dinner—tomorrow the students leave for winter break."

"Well, y'all have a good evening, then." He slapped the hood of the Jeep. "There's snow coming, you know. Better put chains on your tires."

Jayne nodded. "A fairly big storm, from what the weather report said. We might get six or eight inches."

"I heard a foot," Steve said. "I'll drive by and check on you over vacation, be sure everybody's doing well."

"I appreciate it." Jayne lied with a smile, then put the Jeep into gear. Steve's personal interest was getting harder to discourage, though she couldn't help being grateful he'd stepped in this afternoon. Who knew what might have happened if the stranger had kept hold of her?

But he wasn't a stranger now. He had a name—Chris Hammond, grandson to Charlie Hammond. Neither name seemed the least bit familiar. But he had asked if she grew up in Ridgeville, which implied that the person she resembled had lived here. No one else in town had ever mentioned that she looked like someone they knew. Maybe Mr. Hammond was mistaken. Delusional. Drunk.

No, he hadn't been intoxicated. She would have smelled alcohol on his breath, they'd been that close. But Chris Hammond had smelled of soap and fresh air. She'd felt his body heat as she stared up at him for that moment, and sensed the strength in his hand. Strangely, she could still feel his touch, like a band of tender skin around her upper arm.

Though he seemed harsh, with his unruly hair and stubbled cheeks, she'd seen something desperate and sad in his eyes.

Bedroom eyes, her grandmother would have called them, with those lazy, drooping lids. He had a beautiful mouth. His smile would be intriguing. Irresistible.

She was so caught up in her thoughts she almost missed the school entrance, braking hard to avoid cruising right by.

"Since when do you spend time daydreaming about men?" she asked herself, slowing down for the drive through the forest surrounding the Hawkridge School. "You don't have time for romance, even the imaginary kind."

She'd seen three of her teachers fall deeply in love this past year, which probably accounted for the unusual direction her thoughts had taken. As the headmistress of a school housing three hundred girls, each with her own set of problems, plus the staff and faculty required to deal with those students, Jayne rarely had a spare moment to herself. She didn't waste time wondering about a different life or a family of her own. As far as she was concerned, Hawkridge gave her plenty of family and numerous children to look after. Getting involved with a man would simply mean another set of needs to meet.

And the one commodity she would not run out of anytime soon was needs to be met.

Her secretary accosted her as she walked in the door from the staff parking lot. "They've upgraded that snowstorm—we're in for eighteen inches, at least. Starting tomorrow night."

Jayne nodded. "E-mail all the parents and advise them to be here early, so they can be out of the mountains by noon. Ask them to reply at once, and call any you haven't heard from by midnight or can't reach via the Web."

One of the kitchen staff knocked on Jayne's office door before she'd had a chance to take off her coat. "Cook says the market shorted her on the roast beef order. Even accounting for vegetarians, the portions won't stretch to cover all the girls and teachers." The traditional Hawkridge end of term dinner featured roast beef and Yorkshire pudding, so this tragedy assumed immense proportions in the kitchen.

Jayne would have settled for a bowl of soup. But she gave the issue a moment's consideration. "Does she have chicken?"

"Yes, ma'am."

"Ask her to serve chicken to the head table, and present a platter of chicken to the girls' tables along with the beef."

"Yes, ma'am."

Three girls appeared in the outer office, needing to consult with the headmistress over an incident of name-calling and missing bubble bath. Two teachers wanted to discuss a discipline problem. Her secretary returned with the news that one set of parents and one guardian grandfather had called to say they couldn't possibly pick up their daughters before the snow started, and they'd decided to wait the storm out at a luxury hotel in Asheville, an hour away.

Jayne dropped back into her chair. "Terrific. Two more girls for the break. Who are they?"

"Monique Law and Taryn Gage."

"Ah." Monique, a junior, had waged a private war with beer and cocaine since before arriving at Hawkridge two years ago. She managed well as long as she stayed at school, but when she went home, the local crowd and its addictions consumed her. Maybe a snow-enforced vacation at school would help her break the cycle.

Taryn, one of their new students this year, had already been isolated in the infirmary three times as a result of her temper tantrums. The abusive home environment she'd been rescued from explained her rage, but she would have to learn to handle that anger without violence.

Jayne got to her feet as the warning bell for dinner rang.

"I might have more of a challenge on my hands than I realized, staying here alone with seven girls. Do you suppose there's someone else on staff who has no plans for the holiday and would like to help?"

Her secretary pulled a doubtful frown. Jayne nodded. "Right. I didn't think so. Well, I'll worry about that later. First, the faculty procession into dinner."

Standing at the head of the double line of teachers, she allowed herself an appeal for assistance from a higher power. "I could use some backup, here. I can't do everything myself." As she passed between the rows of tables in the dining hall, she saw girls eyeing the platter of chicken with doubt.

"Please," she murmured, with a harried glance heavenward. "At least make the chicken taste good."

"DAMN FOOL, that's what you are, going out in the snow."

Wrapping a scarf around his neck, Chris smiled to himself. "It's not snowing yet, Charlie. The weather report says the snow won't even start till after dark."

"What do they know? I've lived my whole life in these mountains and I tell you it'll be coming down hard and fast by four at the latest." Still with a full head of hair, gray now instead of brown, his grandfather scowled at him.

"Well, I should be back here long before the roads get bad. I just want to ask some questions." He'd told Charlie about yesterday's encounter.

"You showed me that picture on your phone and, yeah, she does look like Juliet. But don't you think I would have heard if Juliet Radcliffe had returned? There's been neither hide nor hair of that girl seen around here since the two of you crashed up on the mountain." The old man grabbed Chris above the elbow and stared at him through round, rimless glasses. "She died that night, Christopher. You've known it for twelve years. Why would you suddenly start doubting?"

Chris patted the chilly fingers. "Because…because I feel it. There's something in this woman's face that I know as well as I know my own. And she's so close to what Juliet might have looked like now. How could that be?"

"They say everybody has a double." Still as tall as ever but on the thin side, after losing fifty pounds to illness, Charlie looked even older than his seventy-eight years.

"Maybe. But in the same North Carolina mountain town? Not likely." He grabbed his helmet off the kitchen table and turned to look at his granddad's worried face. "I'll be back for dinner. Put that meat loaf I bought at the market in the oven with a couple of potatoes. We'll have a good meal, a few beers and watch the ball game on TV. Okay?"

Charlie growled low in his throat. "You're asking for trouble."

That, Chris thought as he fired up the Harley, was probably true. If this Jayne Thomas wasn't who he thought, she might call the Ridgeville police on him. Or the sheriff's department, with Deputy High-and-Mighty. He might end up spending Christmas in jail instead of hanging out with his dying grandfather, storing up memories for when Charlie was gone.

If she *was* Juliet Radcliffe…well, then he had questions to ask. And he wouldn't be leaving her alone until he got the answers.

The drive to Hawkridge School took him fifteen miles along winding, two-lane mountain roads bordered by dark evergreens and bare hardwood trees. Heavy, ash-colored clouds blocked the sun, creating an early twilight. True to Charlie's prediction, snow began to dust the pavement only a couple of miles out of Ridgeville.

Chris grinned as he watched the small white flakes sifting

over the surrounding forest. He'd always loved spending Christmas here in the Smoky Mountains with Charlie. Not every Christmas had been a white one, but he recalled streaking down the hill behind Charlie's cabin on a blue plastic disk sled, hearing Juliet scream as she flew beside him, and then the two of them landing in a tumbled heap in the drifts at the bottom. They'd emerged breathless, crying with laughter, then picked up their sleds and trudged back to the top to do it all over again. Charlie had resorted to bribing them with food to get them inside for even a few minutes.

Chris shook off his memories to realize the snow had picked up and was beginning to coat the road. In the next moment, he saw tall iron gates and a sign flash by—The Hawkridge School.

Damn, he'd missed the entrance.

A set of switchbacks took him farther up the mountain, but then came a long, straight stretch of road suitable for a U-turn. With no traffic in sight, Chris eased the bike around and headed back the way he'd come, slower this time and with his mind on his driving.

The trees along the hairpin curves arched out over the road, blocking most of the snow and also the waning light, until he might as well be driving at night. He'd worn a sweater under his leather jacket, plus a scarf, knit cap and gloves with liners. But even the leather chaps over his jeans didn't cut the frigid wind. His knees and thighs felt like blocks of ice. Inside heavy boots and wool socks, his toes could have been chipped off with an ice pick.

Because of the cold or the darkness, or both, the entrance again came up faster than he expected. Chris started the turn too late, too sharply, just as the tires slipped on the slick asphalt.

He muttered a single swear word.

The bike tilted, then fell over, sliding sideways with Chris's leg pinned underneath. Metal screamed, and he got a glimpse of approaching tree trunks on the other side of empty space. He had just enough time to send up a fervent prayer before wood started to splinter. Then the world went black.

Chapter Two

By midafternoon, the usual bustle in the hallways of the Hawkridge School had dwindled to complete silence. Students, teachers and staff had left the premises as fast as possible, all anxious to be out of the mountains before the snowstorm hit. Only eight individuals remained behind in the mansion—Jayne and the seven girls who had no other place to go.

They'd gathered in a room that students rarely saw, the private library designed for the wife of magnate Horace Ridgely, the builder of Hawkridge Manor. Mrs. Ridgely—Emmeline—had fancied herself a history scholar, and furnished her retreat with comfortably deep leather sofas and chairs surrounded by library tables wide and sturdy enough to hold stacks of books and provide plenty of work space. At each end of the room, walnut bookshelves packed with gold-tooled leather volumes lined the walls from the floor to the fifteen-foot ceiling. On one side, casement windows with diamond panes looked out into a private walled garden where Emmeline might refresh her mind without being disturbed. Across the room, the fireplace could have roasted an ox whole.

The manor had been wired for electricity from the beginning, and the only change made to this room in the last one hundred years was the addition of a discreet mahogany cupboard which, when opened, revealed a large TV screen and all the necessary components for movies and music. As the light failed outside Emmeline's diamond windows, the girls spent the first afternoon of their winter break sprawled across two sofas and four chairs, swooning over handsome actors and cackling at sly jokes.

Jayne had joined them during the first half of the film, but found her attention more attuned to the weather than the antics of a gang of con artists stealing from Las Vegas casinos. Standing by the window, she pulled her sweater close around her as she watched the snowflakes falling faster and harder as the minutes passed. The wind seemed louder and stronger, too.

"It's going to be a real storm, isn't it?" Sarah Minton, a senior who had volunteered to stay and help Jayne with the other girls, came to join her at the window. "It looks kind of scary out there."

Jayne smiled. "But we're safe and sound inside, so we don't have anything to worry about. We're warm and dry and there's lots of food. Lots of firewood, too—I asked Mr. Humphries to leave us a good supply within easy reach." She glanced at the fireplace, where the blaze had gotten low. "Maybe we ought to bring some wood in before—"

"Did you hear that?" Sarah had turned her face toward the garden outside. "It sounded like banging."

"Probably a loose tree branch in the wind." Jayne waited, listening, but didn't hear anything. "I guess—"

The girl held up a hand. "There it is again." This time, in the quiet, Jayne heard the sound, too—a slow, hard pounding.

It stopped, and they both took a deep breath. Then the noise started again.

"That's the front entrance." Jayne crossed toward the door

to the hallway. "You stay here with the girls. I'll return in a few minutes."

But as she turned into the hallway, Sarah was right behind her. "I don't think you should go by yourself."

When Jayne looked back, she saw the six other students had joined them.

"What's happening?"

"Is it time to eat?"

"Where're you going, Ms. Thomas?"

Jayne accepted the unlikely possibility of convincing them to stay behind. "Someone is knocking on the front door. Let's see who's there."

As they proceeded toward the main section of the manor, some of the girls jogged, danced and skipped ahead. But Jayne came to a halt before they could reach the double doors into the foyer. "I want you all behind me once I go through those doors. I'm glad to have your company, but I don't know who is out there, so stay back and out of the way. Understood?"

Seven apprehensive gazes stayed fixed on her face as the girls nodded.

"Good." Jayne pulled open one of the paneled mahogany doors. "Let's go."

She swallowed hard as she crossed the black-and-white marble floor of the huge entrance hall. Past closed doors on the left leading into the dining hall, past the foot of the curved staircase on her right, and the entrance into the administrative office suite just beyond. Finally she stood with her hand on the brass knobs of the double front doors. Taking a deep breath, Jayne squared her shoulders, just as whoever stood outside started pounding again.

"Oh, for heaven's sake!" Using both hands now, she turned the right knob and jerked the panel back.

She noticed the snow first, whirling and slashing in the light from inside and the lamps on the porch. Then she caught a glimpse of blue eyes in a pale face smeared with red. Paint?

Blood. "Sorry," the man confronting her muttered. "Can you…" he swayed from side to side "…help?"

Before the word ended, he pitched forward, right into Jayne's arms.

At her back, several of the girls screamed. Jayne staggered under the man's weight, reaching out by instinct to hold him. Though she struggled to stay upright, he bore her down to the floor, collapsing with most of her body underneath his. He was sopping wet. And freezing.

"My God, he's heavy." As Sarah moved to shut the door, Jayne pulled her arms free and braced herself against the hard floor with her hands behind her. She could hardly budge, pinned as she was with the man's head on her chest and the rest of him draped over her.

She struggled to organize her thoughts. "Sarah, take Taryn and Yolanda up to the infirmary and bring back the stretcher. You may use the elevator coming down," she called as they went running up the stairs. "Just hurry!"

A glance at the agitated faces of the other girls told her she had to get them out of the way and occupied. "You four are the dinner crew."

When the moans died down, she continued. "Let's keep it simple, since we've got an emergency to deal with. Haley and Monique, make grilled cheese sandwiches. At least twelve of them. Selena and Beth, heat up soup in a big pot on the stove. We'll need some hot tea, too, for Mr. Two Tons, here."

She tried to shift, and groaned at her lack of success. The girls gave nervous laughs. "Just make something we can eat when we get this guy settled. That's all I ask."

They returned the way they'd come, and Jayne let her head fall back, trying to ease the tension in her neck and shoulders. "Hurry," she murmured to Sarah, Taryn and Yolanda. "Or I may never walk again."

As if in answer, wheels squeaked somewhere beyond the top of the grand curved staircase. "We're on our way," Sarah called. "Had some trouble figuring out how to operate the stretcher. Be there in a minute."

"Whew." Jayne sighed in relief, then gasped as the body lying on top of her moved.

"What the hell...?" His words were slurred, his voice hoarse. "Where am I?" He jerked to the side, off of her, then propped himself on one elbow and stared at Jayne. Comprehension dawned in those sky-blue eyes. "Did I pass out on top of you? Are you okay?"

Before she could answer, he tried to lift his other hand to his head. Swearing, he fell backward instead, and lay flat on the floor, his face twisted in pain.

Jayne shifted to her knees beside him. "What's wrong? Is your arm broken?"

"Dislocated," he growled between bared teeth. "Shoulder."

The squeak of wheels announced the arrival of the stretcher.

"What can we do?" Sarah asked, breathing hard.

Jayne considered the white-faced man on the floor. "Yolanda and Taryn, you two go down to the staff kitchen and see if the girls there need help with supper. Sarah and I can manage here."

"But—" Yolanda started.

Looking up, Jayne lifted an eyebrow. "Surely you're not going to argue. I believe I made the rules clear at our meeting this afternoon." She used her quietest, most intimidating head-mistress voice.

"Yes, ma'am." Haley Farrish, a ninth-grader, elbowed the other girl in the side. "Come on. We can get some chips. I'm starving."

Yolanda Warner hesitated, her lower lip stuck out in a pout. As a junior, she probably thought she should be allowed to help. But when the man on the floor groaned and struggled to sit up, panic chased away her self-importance. In the next moment, she and Haley disappeared through the office doorway.

Jayne scrambled to her feet and motioned for Sarah to come to the man's uninjured side. "Let us help you up," she told him. "We'll lift under your arms—"

"God, no." Holding his injured left arm against his side with his other hand, he had somehow managed to maneuver himself to his knees. "Just give me a second." He stayed there for much longer than a second, head bowed, his harsh breaths the only sound in the immense space of the entry hall.

Then his right knee jerked up, he planted his foot against the marble floor and drove himself to stand. He swayed, and Jayne stepped closer, arms out. Sarah, on his other side, did the same.

But this time he didn't collapse. Blowing out a deep breath, the man turned slowly to face Jayne.

His eyes were bloodshot, his hair hanging in wet tangles, his face frozen in lines of agony. For the first time, though, she recognized her stalker from the previous day in town.

"Remember me? I'm Chris Hammond," he said, his voice still ragged. "I came here to find out where you've been the last twelve years.

"And why the hell you're lying about who you are."

THE HEADMISTRESS DROPPED her jaw till Chris could practically see her tonsils. Her dark, straight brows drew together over eyes the exact hazel color he remembered. He would swear he knew the shape of every freckle on her nose. Oh, yeah, she was lying, all right.

"Well?" He dragged in a breath against the agony searing his shoulder. "What's with the fake name?"

She gave her head a quick shake. "I don't know what you're talking about."

"I'm talking about your real name—Juliet Radcliffe. If you were trying to hide, Ridgeville wasn't the smartest spot to choose."

"I'm not hiding." She looked across him at the girl still standing with her arms out, ready to catch him if he fell. Or maybe tackle him if he attacked. "Sarah, go check on the girls. If the food is ready, you all should eat."

"But—"

A lift of the headmistress's right eyebrow stifled the protest and Sarah disappeared behind the curving staircase.

Chris waited until the woman turned back to him. "Girls? I don't remember any other girls."

"This is a school," she said, letting her effort to stay patient show. "There are students here."

He shrugged, which was a mistake. Pain narrowed the world to whirling white dots in front of his eyes. He didn't know if he'd be sick or pass out. Maybe throw up, then pass out.

Her hand closed around the elbow of his good arm. "Look, we can settle identities later. You need medical attention. I'll drive you—"

His laugh set off another spasm of anguish. "You're not driving anywhere," he said, when he could stop gasping. "The roads are slicker than a skating rink."

"Is it really that bad?"

Chris snorted. "How do you think I got in this shape?" She

just stared at him, a bemused look on her face. "My bike slid out from under me down on the highway, that's how. I landed at your front gate, with the Harley wrapped around a nearby tree."

"You walked up here from the highway? After an accident?" Now both her hands gripped his arm, the only warm spot on his entire body. He could almost see the wheels in her head turning, preparing to deal with the situation. "We've got to get you taken care of. What can we do about your shoulder?"

He wasn't surprised at the question—Juliet would know he'd been dealing with this issue since he was fifteen. "Just take hold of my wrist. Come on," he said when she hesitated. "You've done this before."

She shook her head, but moved her hands to his left wrist. "You have me confused with someone else."

"Not likely." He forced his numb fingers to wrap around her wrist, linking them together. "Bend the arm to my waist. Right angle." He couldn't stop the hiss as she followed directions. "Okay. Hold tight, now. Brace yourself for a jerk."

"I believe we've already met," she murmured.

Chris felt his lips twitch with the urge to grin in response. But in the next moment the slight curve of her full lips straightened.

"Are you sure this will work?"

"Hell, no." Chris took a breath, turned his head, then used his legs to drag all of his weight to the left. His shoulder muscles screamed, he groaned…and the ball of his shoulder slipped back into the socket.

"Ahhh." He couldn't hold back the sigh of relief. "That's better."

Still cradling his hand and wrist, she gazed at him. "You're okay?"

"If you don't count the crashing headache, plus a full load of cuts and bruises, I'm great."

"You do have blood on your face." She reached a hand toward his cheek. "Where did it—"

But Chris pulled away before her fingertips made contact, taking a long step backward and putting as much distance between them as he could manage. "I'll take inventory later. Did you say something about food?"

She looked stunned for a second, but then nodded. "Yes. You can get cleaned up in the staff restroom, and then we'll get dinner. Just soup and grilled cheese sandwiches," she said over her shoulder, heading in the same direction the girl, Sarah, had gone. "I hope that's okay."

"I'll be happier if you have a beer to go with it." Though Chris had never been inside Hawkridge Manor, what he'd seen so far lived up to the stories he'd heard. The marble floor and mahogany paneling of the two-story entry hall rivaled some palaces he'd photographed in other countries.

"Here's the restroom." The headmistress stopped beside a cherry paneled door with the appropriate gender sign. "The kitchen is on the right, three doors down. Join us when you're ready."

She continued in that direction, but stopped when he said, "Does that mean no beer?"

Without looking back, she said, "Strong coffee is the best I can do."

Chris pushed the bathroom door open with his good shoulder. "Without beer," he mourned, "this will be a bitch of a storm."

The restroom behind the old-fashioned door was modern and convenient, but the surroundings did nothing to make him feel better. Indigo-colored bruises from his helmet had started showing up on his cheeks and chin, along with a cut on his right jaw that had bled like crazy until his circulation slowed with the cold.

Still, he'd survived, which he wouldn't have bet on at the time. One of those tree trunks had come damn close to his head.

His leather jacket was a total loss—ripped at both shoulder seams, with the finish on the back sanded off by the asphalt pavement. He eased it off his shoulders and let it fall down his arms straight into the trash can.

The sweater he'd worn inside the jacket was still in good shape, but the collar of the shirt underneath had been soaked with blood, so he stripped to the waist. Pain from his dislocated shoulder stabbed at him with every move, and tomorrow it would spread across his chest and back, he knew. A glance at the mirror showed him the bruises outlining his ribs, not to mention the outlines of the ribs themselves. The months in Africa had been pretty rough. His shoulders had gotten bony, and his jeans hung loose on his hips. He'd really been looking forward to that meat loaf with Charlie tonight.

Not bothering to stifle his groans, Chris pulled the sweater back over his head, then wet his fingers and ran them through his hair to tame it. The ruined chaps had protected his jeans from major damage, except for being wet to the knees with snowmelt. He thought he looked decent enough for a sandwich with a bunch of schoolkids.

After food and some of that strong coffee, though, he planned to corner Juliet Radcliffe and drag the truth out of her. He would find out what was behind this stupid innocent act of hers if it took all night.

More important, he'd find out why she'd disappeared. And why she'd let him spend the last twelve years believing he'd killed her.

JAYNE ENTERED THE STAFF kitchen to find her seven students staring at a stack of charcoal bricks in place of the sandwiches.

Monique threw her hands in the air. "I can't cook. And I shouldn't have to. Meals are part of the deal here, right?" She stalked to the couch and plopped down, with her arms folded high across her chest and the bright beads on her many black braids clicking as they bounced. "I'm not gonna starve, either. Somebody had better make me something to eat."

Jayne nodded. "That's fine. You don't have to cook. You can work with the cleanup crew after every meal."

"No way." Her skin, usually a soft shade of creamed coffee, darkened with an angry flush.

"Those are the rules," Sarah said, without prompting from Jayne. "Staying at school over winter break means helping out with the chores. I'm not cooking extra food for somebody who won't do her share." She looked around at the other girls, who were nodding in response.

But Monique didn't give in. "I don't care. I'll just go into town with that dude when he leaves."

"I'm not leaving anytime soon," a masculine voice answered. "You'll get pretty hungry."

The eight of them gasped in unison at the intrusion, then turned to see Chris Hammond leaning against the frame of the kitchen door.

"My bike is wrapped around a tree down by the road," he continued. "And the snow's a good six inches deep by now, with no sign of stopping." He walked to the table and pulled out the chair on the end. "Ladies, I hope you don't mind if I sit down. It's been a long afternoon."

Without waiting for their agreement, he lowered himself into the chair. From the way his face whitened as he bent his legs, Jayne guessed he'd suffered more than a dislocated shoulder in the crash. He needed food and warm liquids.

"Good point," she said briskly, moving to pour a mug of coffee. "Girls, this is Mr. Hammond, our guest." Each of the girls introduced herself in turn. "Since no one is going anywhere tonight, let's give the grilled cheese sandwiches another try. How's the soup coming?" She glanced into the pot, then at the knobs of the stove. "Turn up the heat, get it almost to a boil," she told Selena. "Beth, set the table with plates and bowls. Yolanda can figure out what everyone wants to drink."

Jayne put the coffee down beside the intruder's left hand. "Sugar and cream?"

He shook his head and brought the mug to his lips, then managed to sigh as he swallowed. "That's good," he murmured. "Thanks."

"Let me know when you want a refill." She left him alone as she supervised the dinner preparations, making sure the sandwiches emerged from the pan unscorched, the soup didn't boil over and there were napkins on the table. Making sure, as well, that she didn't stare at him, didn't notice—again— the sharp blue of his eyes under thick, spiky lashes, or his sensuous lower lip, or the breadth of his shoulders.

Where in the world was her mind wandering, in the midst of all these teenaged girls? Maybe adolescent angst was contagious.

With golden sandwiches piled high on a plate and chicken noodle soup ladled into nine bowls, Jayne told the girls to sit down and eat. When the flurry of movement subsided, two empty places remained—one beside Chris Hammond and the other at the far end, facing him. Over on the couch, Monique still pouted. So Jayne had the choice of sitting next to him or facing him as if they were parents on either end of the family table.

Avoiding the domestic image, she sat down in the chair at

his left hand. She could pour more coffee that way, and monitor his conversation with the girls.

After all, what kind of man did they have stranded with them tonight? He might be a pedophile, for all she knew. He'd stalked her all over Ridgeville just yesterday. And he'd said—she'd blocked the memory in the urgency of the moment—he'd said he'd come to find out why she was lying about her name and about not knowing him. The very idea meant he was delusional, at least. He'd clearly mistaken her for someone else. At the worst, he might actually be mentally unstable.

But she couldn't have left him out in the snow, injured and bleeding, even if she'd had a choice. Which she hadn't, because he'd fallen in the door without waiting for permission. Was he dangerous? Would she and the girls all be murdered in their beds?

"What are you worrying about?"

She snapped her head around to look at him. "I—I'm not worrying. Just eating."

Chris Hammond gave a lopsided smile. "Except you haven't picked up your spoon or taken a sandwich. You're staring off into space with that little crease between your eyebrows you always get when you're worried. And you're wringing your hands in your lap."

Jayne immediately relaxed her fingers. "I was just thinking about the storm." The flush from that lie crept up her neck under her turtleneck shirt. "Do you know how much snow they're predicting?"

He took a crunching bite of his sandwich and swallowed. "My granddad was predicting a blizzard as I left this afternoon. Maybe I should have believed him."

"Is he a weather forecaster?"

"Just an old mountaineer." Chris Hammond turned his head to lock his gaze with hers. "As you should remember."

Her denial was overwhelmed by Yolanda's shout from the other end of the table. "Hey, Ms. Thomas, can we go sledding after dinner?"

A chorus of cheers greeted the question.

"In the dark? Absolutely not." Jayne shook her head. "You can play in the snow tomorrow."

"There are lights all around outside," Yolanda pointed out. "It's practically daylight out there."

"Yeah, those lights shine in my window every night." Monique had finally allowed hunger to win, and had taken her place at the table. "I should know."

"The best sledding hill doesn't have lights," Jayne told them. "There's a little bowl on the other side of the woods, off the hiking path to Hawk's Ridge. We call it The Nest. Girls usually try to see who can go down one side the fastest and then come up the other side the farthest." She shrugged. "Of course, if you'd rather settle for the tame little bumps around here instead of spending several hours in The Nest, that's up to you."

"Masterful strategy," the man beside her murmured.

The girls around the table debated for a few seconds. "The Nest sounds cool," Yolanda announced. "How early can we leave?"

"How early do you plan to get up?" Jayne pushed back her chair and stood. "While you're deciding, let's get the kitchen cleaned up. Dishes to the sink, paper to the trash and the leftovers in the fridge. Monique, you're washing."

"I know, I know." Rolling her eyes, the girl went to the sink and began running water. "Get over here and help me, Haley. You didn't do much with dinner, either."

"I opened the soup cans," Haley protested. But she found a dish towel and prepared to dry the wet dishes.

"Wipe the table down," Jayne reminded them, "while I—"

A big fist closed around her upper arm. Chris Hammond had gotten to his feet. "I need to talk to you." His set face matched the steel in his tone…and his grip. "Now."

Sarah came up on Jayne's other side. "Ms. Thomas? Are you okay?"

"I'm not going to murder or rape her," Chris Hammond said irritably.

Pale blond hair and light blue eyes might give the impression that Sarah would be timid, but she didn't flinch in the face of Chris Hammond's temper. Jayne put her free hand on the girl's arm. "I'm fine. There's something Mr. Hammond and I need to get straightened out. I'll show him where he can sleep tonight and be back here in a few minutes."

As she stepped past him, the grip on her arm fell away. Jayne walked down the hallway to the private door of her office without looking back, certain he would follow. She motioned him inside, then shut the door and leaned back against it, refusing to let him believe she was scared of being alone with him.

Although, in truth, she was terrified.

"All right, Mr. Hammond, you've got what you want—complete privacy with no possible intervention from the police, the girls or anyone else. What in the world do you have to say to me?"

Chapter Three

Chris took his time examining the office. More wood paneling and a wall of bookshelves surrounded a huge desk with brass handles. Leather armchairs and a brocade sofa faced each other on an Oriental carpet. Original oil paintings and velvet drapes at the windows bespoke money and prestige.

"Very nice," he said crisply, turning to face the headmistress again. "Looks like a cushy job. One you wouldn't want to lose."

"Yes." She didn't dress to impress, which suggested she was very comfortable with the power she held. Posed with her shoulders against the door, wearing navy blue slacks and white sneakers, a navy sweater and white turtleneck, she looked casual and confident. But he could sense the tension in her body.

"Is that the reason you won't tell the truth?"

"What truth? What could I possibly be lying about?"

Chris set his jaw. "Your name, for starters. Not Jayne Thomas, but Juliet Radcliffe."

"I have never heard that name before in my life. And it certainly isn't mine. You have me confused with someone else."

He sat on the edge of the big desk. "So where do you come from?"

Her shoulders relaxed a fraction. "About fifty miles south. My grandmother lived near Nantahala. She raised me."

"Not your parents?"

"Our house burned down when I was seven. They were killed trying to bring out my little brother."

"That's quite a tragedy."

She gave him a dirty look. "Don't be so sympathetic."

"Sorry. But I don't understand why you would make up a background like that when you've got a legitimate past to call on. With me."

She took a step forward. "You have to believe me. I've never heard of Juliet Radcliffe." Her voice had softened, lowered, as if she were pacifying a wild animal. "You and I met for the first time yesterday."

"Charlie says different."

"Charlie?" She stared at him with a puzzled look. "Your grandfather? How would he know?"

Chris took out his cell phone. "Not much quality in these gadgets, but you get a general idea. I snapped your picture yesterday in town. Charlie said he would have known you anywhere." He pushed a few buttons and called up the photo, then held up the phone screen for her to see.

She gave it a brief glance. "Charlie, the 'old mountaineer'? At least he's got the excuses of age and bad eyesight. You, I'm afraid, are just plain wrong." Turning her back to him, she reached for the doorknob. "Now that we've got that settled, I think the best place for you to sleep is—"

"The hell we have." Chris strode forward, grabbed her forearm with his good hand and pulled her around to face him, while shutting the door with a single kick. Then he gripped her other elbow, ignoring the spear of pain through his shoulder. "I learned every inch of your body when we were seventeen."

She stopped struggling and stared at him, mouth open.

He nodded. "You have a birthmark on your left hip, red and shaped like a boot." Her gasp made him smile. "Oh, yeah, I've seen it. I've kissed it. Want to tell me now that I'm plain wrong?"

Before his next heartbeat, the lights went out.

IN THE ABSOLUTE BLACKNESS, the girls started screaming.

"Dear God." Jayne whirled, felt for the doorknob and flung open the panel. "Sarah! Monique!" Out in the dark hallway, she started running. "It's okay, girls," she called. "Everything's okay."

"No generator?" Chris Hammond asked from behind her.

"There is. I don't know why it's not kicking on."

Outside the kitchen, she ran into a bumbling, sobbing huddle of teenage girls. Stretching out her arms, she touched as many of them as she could reach. "Calm down, everybody. We're okay. Everybody is okay. Our eyes are adjusting. We'll be able to see soon. Shh. Shh. Just relax."

Gradually, the sobs were replaced by sniffles. Jayne herded the girls into the library, where embers glowed red in the fireplace.

"We've got plenty of flashlights," she told them, "one for each of you, at least. Thousands of batteries. We'll build up the fire and be warm and cozy."

"What happened?" Taryn's voice still quivered. "Why did the lights go out?"

"I don't know." Jayne carried a plastic tub of flashlights and batteries from the storeroom into the library.

"Isn't there a backup generator?" Sarah started handing out the torches. "Doesn't it switch on automatically?"

"That's the plan." Jayne stood back as the girls began playing with their lights. "I don't know why it didn't work."

"Can't we call somebody to come fix it?"

At the window, Jayne looked out into a white curtain of snow. "I don't think anyone can get out from town tonight." She picked up the nearby phone and was relieved to hear the dial tone. "I'll call first thing tomorrow morning."

Red-haired Haley raised her hand. "Ms. Thomas, who's taking care of the horses? If Miss Ruth Ann can't get here, are they going to starve in the snow?" A computer genius with a history of anorexia and several arrests for hacking into business systems, Haley had started riding lessons this fall.

"We're lucky in that regard. Ms. Granger had already planned to spend the vacation with her husband and daughter in Ireland. She left our horses with different friends in the area to be cared for with their animals. They're fine."

"Whew." Haley sat back in her chair. "I'm glad."

As the girls relaxed, Jayne had the chance to realize Chris Hammond wasn't in the room. With her flashlight clenched in suddenly clammy fingers, she checked the kitchen, the storerooms and even the men's restroom without finding him.

For a few moments, she stood in the hallway outside the library, considering Hammond's strange disappearance. Where had he gone? Why?

A sudden gust of cold wind swirled around her legs. The beam of her torch showed Jayne that the outside door, locked as usual, was propped open a few inches. Chris Hammond had left the building. Would he come back? With a weapon this time? She didn't know him, had no reason to trust him.

Maybe she *should* call the sheriff's office. They might need help up here, after all….

In the next minute, the door opened all the way and the man in question stepped inside. The beam from his flashlight hit her square in the face, then dropped immediately.

Jayne kept hers high. "Where have you been?"

"Do you mind?" He brought his hand up to shield his eyes. She didn't move. "Why did you go outside?"

"I thought I would find and check out the generator, see if I could get it running."

"Oh." She lowered the flashlight. "What's wrong with it?"

"I can't tell. When's the last time you needed it?"

"Never, in the three years I've been here. But we get yearly maintenance from the company."

"Then you'll have to ask them what went wrong. It's dead out there, though. No chance of power for tonight." He pulled the door firmly closed behind him. "What about water?"

"We're supplied by the town reservoir, so we should be okay. If that water failed, we could switch over to the original Hawkridge supply, from a lake high in the mountains. We won't have to melt snow to drink."

His teeth flashed in the dark. "And are we taking cold showers?"

"Our water heaters are gas, so we'll have hot water for showers and washing up. Thank goodness."

"Things could definitely be worse." He tilted his head and looked at her quizzically. "So, do you still suspect I'm an ax murderer?"

"Yes." Without smiling, Jayne turned and went back into the library. The girls had settled around the fireplace, thanks to Sarah's brilliant discoveries—marshmallows and coat hangers.

"Are there chocolate bars and graham crackers?" Taryn licked white goo off her fingers. "We could make s'mores."

Jayne didn't want to take on another project tonight. "We'll look for those tomorrow in the daylight."

A general protest rose from the crowd around the fireplace, expanding to take in the weather, the lack of power and entertainment options and the miserable state of their adolescent world in general. The whines and complaints came at Jayne as only the most recent coating on a snowball of stress and tension that had been rolling downhill for the last two days, growing larger with every moment and now barreling straight at her.

She dropped into the nearest chair, her hands clamped tight together. In a minute she would regain control.

"Hey, girls! Shut up!" The shout actually echoed in the large room. Through the silence that followed, all eyes turned to the source of the command.

"That's better." Standing just inside the library door, Chris Hammond surveyed each of them in turn, one eyebrow lifted in sardonic question over those steel-blue eyes. "Is this a bunch of five-year-olds? You sound like it."

Resentment flared on several faces. Yolanda opened her mouth to speak.

Chris held up a hand. "No excuses. This is far from the worst place you could be holed up during a blizzard. From what I heard at dinner, most of you chose to stay at school over the holiday."

Yolanda's mouth shut.

"Right now you're warm, there's food and drink and you've got company. You could be in the Middle East, holed up in a cave, looking for an enemy you can't see even in the daytime. No fire allowed, only water to drink, and freeze-dried food from a bag for Christmas dinner."

"Have you done that?" Taryn asked, curling one of her frizzy brown pigtails around her finger.

"I've traveled with the soldiers carrying the guns. My weapon of choice is a camera."

A photojournalist, Jayne thought, as her hands began to relax. *Interesting.*

"Can we see your pictures?"

He dragged a ladderback chair near the fire. "Didn't bring my camera on this trip."

"Do you work for a newspaper?"

"I usually freelance—I come up with projects and then look for an editor who's interested."

Beth Steinman, whose expensive and stylish haircut branded her a resident of Manhattan, asked, "Have you ever published pictures in the *New York Times?*"

"Three articles last year."

"Wow."

"How about the *L.A. Times?*" Selena Hernandez represented the West Coast at Hawkridge.

"I just sold them a piece, and they asked for more."

"Cool!"

His genuine smile was just as nice as Jayne had expected. "I have a blog, too. I post pictures and articles on *The View from Here.*"

"So we could find you online?" The girls sat up in excitement, then all fell back to their usual slumps. "No electricity, no Internet."

"Something else to look forward to when the power returns." Jayne got to her feet. "With the heating off, we'll have to sleep near the fire. We're going to the dormitory now so each of you can change into pajamas, robes and slippers. A scarf or a soft hat might be a good idea—you'll stay warmer if you sleep with your head covered. Then you can bring sheets, blankets and pillows back down and we'll get set up for the night."

The predictable protests ensued.

"So early?"

"I'm not sleepy."

"I stay up till midnight, at least."

"I can't sleep without my tunes."

Jayne held up her hands for silence. "We've got a school full of books," she reminded them. "Also games, puzzles, paint kits…you can choose whatever you want to do."

The walk through the dark halls by flashlight and the pajama-clad procession back to the library, dragging bedding and stuffed animals, only seemed to drive the energy level higher. A pillow fight erupted and threatened to soar out of control until Jayne pointed out what could happen if flying pillows caught fire. Hunger struck next, and no one seemed to be satisfied with cold candy, cheese and crackers. The absence of a microwave oven brought tempers and tears almost to the breaking point.

Without thinking, Jayne glanced at Chris Hammond, standing at the door observing the chaos. He nodded once, then gave another of those shouts, which again created instant silence. With a hand motion, he turned the room back over to her.

She cleared her throat. "Okay. If you can all settle down, get your bed made, such as it is, and sit on it, I will make hot chocolate for everybody. But you have to be calm. Cooking on the fire isn't easy."

"You can cook on the fire?" Beth looked skeptical.

"As long as people aren't wrestling and throwing things nearby."

"Then what?" Taryn always managed to ask the hardest questions.

Yolanda threw her pillow on the floor. "Yeah, how are we gonna get to sleep without TV or music?"

"As I said, there are books—" Jayne began.

"Or," Chris Hammond offered, "I could tell you a story."

"A STORY?" Yolanda, the tall girl with a boyish haircut and espresso skin, glared at him. "You think we look like little kids?"

Selena from L.A. snorted. "I hate those stupid fairy tales."

But the blonde, Sarah, asked, "What kind of story?"

He settled into the chair near the fire. "It's not a fairy tale, by any means. Not even fiction. This is a true story."

"About who?"

He lifted his eyebrow. "What about *Ms. Thomas's* instructions?" In the scurry to get their bedding straightened out, the girls didn't notice his sarcastic emphasis on her name.

The headmistress did, but chose to ignore him as she carried a stockpot of milk to the fireplace and set it on a three-legged iron stand above a small pile of coals she'd raked forward, out of the blaze.

Then she sat on the hearth, too, legs curled underneath her, to stir the milk as it heated. Gradually, the girls quieted down on top of their blankets and turned their attention back to Chris.

"So?" Monique, the troublemaker from dinner, glared at him with a skeptical curl to her lips. "What's this story about?"

"A boy," Chris Hammond told them. "And a girl."

A raspberry sound effect greeted his announcement. "Hansel and Gretel?" That was one of the quieter girls whose name he didn't know, a redhead with green eyes.

"I don't like fairy tales." Selena began rubbing lotion into her hands and arms.

"Are they vampires?" The one with pigtails clutched a pink stuffed rabbit. "I like vampire stories."

"No, not vampires." He rolled his eyes. "And not zombies, either. Or demons or whatever other unnatural, unreal creatures you pretend stalk the earth." Bloodsucking sounded tame compared to some of the horrors he'd seen humans perpetrate on their own kind. "Just a boy and a girl."

"So what's the big deal?"

He hadn't expected this to be such a hard sell. "Well, they

grew up together. Had lots of adventures. Fell in love." More derisive sound effects. "Then he killed her."

The girls gasped. Chris glanced at the headmistress, saw her sitting upright, motionless, staring at him. Good. He'd gotten her attention.

The redhead broke the silence. "Why'd he do that? How?"

"That's part of the story. If you want to hear it, you have to settle down."

Mumbling and grumbling ensued, as the seven girls tucked and rolled themselves into their makeshift beds on the plush Persian carpet near the fire. Chris shifted a little in his chair, trying to get comfortable; between bruises and scrapes and a pulled shoulder, every inch of his body hurt in one way or another. He could hardly wait to lie down, even on a bare floor.

First, though, he would tell his story. *Their* story. The Juliet he knew couldn't hold out against the truth spoken aloud. This Jayne mask she was wearing would crack at some point as she relived their time together. Then he would corner her, in front of seven witnesses, if necessary, and get the answers he needed.

"So," he began, "they met the first time when they were thirteen years old."

The pink rabbit person popped her head up. "What were their names?"

"Juliet," he said. The headmistress narrowed her eyes, and he thought for a second she would stop him from telling the story.

When she didn't say anything, he looked at the girls again.

"Juliet and…" Yolanda prompted.

"And…" What name could he use for himself? What would impress these girls?

"Romeo?" Monique snorted. "That's so lame."

"Nobody's named Romeo these days," Selena added. "Except dogs."

"Chase," Chris decided. "Juliet and Chase." He thought it sounded like a soap opera couple. But when no protest greeted the announcement, he continued. "It was three days before Christmas...."

His grandfather had sent him to the general store for nails to fix a fence. Chase thought he'd get a bag of chips and a soda with the change from the ten dollar bill Granddad had given him.

Juliet was just wasting time, prowling the store aisles because she was tired of sitting around at her grandmother's house, pretending to read.

It was just her bad luck that Chase glanced over as she dropped the candy bar in her coat pocket. Juliet didn't even realize she'd been caught until he spoke into her ear from behind, "Gotcha!"

She jumped and looked around to see if anybody had heard him. "Shut up!" she hissed. "Keep your mouth closed and I'll give you half."

He shook his head. "Shoplifting's a crime."

"Like he'll even notice it's gone." She nodded toward the man at the counter, who just happened to be a good friend of Chase's granddad.

"Why don't you just buy it?" She was pretty, which accounted for what he said next. "I'll buy it for you."

"That's no fun." She turned and started walking toward the door, pretending to look at the dish towels and pots on the shelves.

Chase watched her go, arguing with himself even while he noticed her long reddish hair shine in the light coming through the high windows. On the one hand, he should tell the store manager. That was the right thing to do. Only problem was, he'd look like a wuss and she'd hate him forever. At thirteen, he wasn't sure which was worse.

While he was still debating, Juliet slipped out the door without a glance in the manager's direction. He didn't even notice her. She'd gotten away with stealing.

When Chase brought his nails and chips and soda to the counter, he found himself talking to Mr. Fletcher, the manager, who'd known him since he was about three years old. And he started feeling guilty for letting the girl get away with her crime. A thirty-five cent candy bar was no big deal. Still, Mr. Fletcher was a nice guy.

At the last minute, he said, "I almost forgot—I bought that girl a candy bar. A Snickers. Add that in."

He left feeling more like Galahad than that Quisling guy they'd talked about in school.

Once out on the sidewalk, he looked around and saw her slouched on a bench just up the street, slowly eating the candy bar. Chase went to sit beside her, opened his chips and took a swig of his drink. But he didn't say anything.

Finally, she said, "You bought it, didn't you?"

He just nodded, pretending to finish chewing a chip.

"Wuss," she told him.

From the floor in front of the fireplace, the seven Hawk-ridge girls groaned.

Chris grinned. "You can't win when it comes to girls."

Monique snorted. "Get on with the story." She glanced at the headmistress's disapproving face. "Please."

"Right. So then…"

She gave a sideways glance. "What do you do around here for fun, anyway?"

"Besides shoplifting?"

Juliet jabbed him in the side with her elbow.

"There's plenty to do in the snow." He glanced up at the sky—it had been a warm winter and they were only wearing sweaters. "Not much if there's no snow."

She sighed and raised her arms in the air. "Why am I here? What possible point is there to Christmas in this hick town?"

He finished his chips, balled the bag and tossed it toward the trash can, praying for a basket. But the bag bounced off the rim and fell on the sidewalk. Feeling his ears heat up, he retrieved the trash and dropped it in the container.

As he sat down again, though, he managed to casually turn his body toward her and prop his elbow on the back of the seat. In a few minutes he would stretch out his arm behind her shoulders. If he was really lucky, some of that shiny red-brown hair would brush his hand.

"I'm Chase," he told her.

"Juliet." She crushed the candy wrapper and pitched it at the trash can, where it landed without a sound.

"Are you from around here?" he asked, to distract from his hot, red cheeks.

"No way. I live in New York." She tossed her hair back over her shoulder. If he'd had his arm stretched out, he could have caught some across his palm. "Manhattan, where there's shopping and music, plays and people and a hundred things to do."

"So why'd you come to the mountains?"

"My grandmother. She's sick and she said she wanted to see me before she dies." Juliet rolled her eyes. "She never wanted to see me before. I barely know the old bat, but I'm forced to spend a whole week trapped in the middle of nowhere." Head bowed, the girl sat and sulked.

Chase took the chance to lay his arm across the back of the bench. "I'm here for the whole winter break. Got here on the twentieth and I'm stuck for three weeks."

Finally, she seemed a little curious. "You're not from here? Where do you live?"

"Philadelphia."

"So you're a prisoner, too."

Chase shook his head. "Nah. In Philly I'm the prisoner. I get free when I come to visit my granddad."

"Parental marriage issues?"

"Big time. At least here nobody's fighting World War III. My granddad's a pretty cool old guy."

She tossed that hair again, but it missed his hand. "My parents basically live on different planets. My granddads both died before I was born and this is the first time I've met the grandmother here. The one in New York, my dad's mother, is a first-class bitch."

"You should meet my granddad. You'd like him."

Juliet bounced off the bench to her feet. "Okay, let's go."

Chase stood up more slowly. "You want to go see him? Now?"

"Sure. Why not?"

"I…" He couldn't think of why not, except… "I only have one bike."

"Cool," she said. "You can ride me on the handlebars."

And that's what they did. Juliet sat in front of him and Chase pedaled for all he was worth. Going up the hills nearly killed him and he nearly killed her as they flew down the slopes. Good thing his granddad lived only three miles outside of town. Chase didn't know if his heart would last any farther.

* * *

When he stopped at the end of the long dirt driveway, Juliet dropped off the front of the bike and looked around at his granddad's place. "Beverly Hillbillies, anyone?"

He surveyed the junk-cluttered yard with a smile. "Yeah, Granddad likes to tinker with engines, and he's not much on mowing grass or pulling weeds." Chase stomped up the rickety steps to the front porch. "Inside's better, 'cause he has a lady come clean every week. Except for his workshop, which is a danger zone all by itself."

He held back the screen door and pushed the front door open. "Come on in."

"Don't mind if I do." She stepped past him, brushing her shoulder against his chest and her hip against his legs.

Chase felt every cell in his body go on alert. He was a goner from that moment on.

Chris doubted any of the girls heard that last part. All of them appeared to have fallen asleep, which was exactly what he'd intended.

Jayne Thomas stirred in her chair. "That was quite an opening chapter." He could barely see her in the near-dark, and her voice sounded calm. Had he not stirred a single memory? "Do you include 'novelist' on your résumé? 'Storyteller,' perhaps?"

"No. I get paid to tell the truth."

She didn't respond, and he knew he'd failed. At the same time, he realized how exhausted he was. "Anywhere in particular you want me to sleep?" He winced as he stood up. His muscles had petrified while he sat. "As far away from this room as possible, I assume."

"Well…" Her hesitation told him she approved that suggestion. "This is the only working fireplace. The rest of the building will be very, very cold."

Chris shrugged a shoulder—the wrong one, but he swallowed the groan. "Doesn't matter. I've slept in colder places." He looked at the fire, now reduced to glowing red embers. "I'll put a couple of logs on and bring more in. But you'll have to keep it stoked overnight, or you'll all be freezing in the morning along with me."

She still didn't move. "Yes."

When he brought the wood in from outside, Juliet—Jayne—was standing near the fireplace, in case he tried something with one of the girls, Chris guessed. After stacking the logs carefully on the hearth, he straightened up. "I'll grab some blankets from the infirmary, if that's okay. In fact, maybe I'll just sack out on a bed in there." He sent her a grin. "At this point, a mattress might be a better deal than mere heat."

He thought he saw her smile. "That could be true."

As he went to the door, the beam of her flashlight came up beside him, then went ahead of him out into the hallway. "The infirmary is on the second floor," she said. "On the right."

"I remember, more or less." He started toward the double doors to the entry hall, surprised to find her walking beside him. "You were waiting for the girls to bring a stretcher down."

"I thought you were unconscious all that time."

"When I land in a good place, I stay there."

The headmistress didn't say anything to that.

Chris put his hand on the door panel, but shifted to face her before he pushed. Dim light reflected from the polished hardwood, revealing her face only in the contours of shadows. Round cheeks, delicate chin. Plump, full lips, parted slightly.

She was Juliet, he knew it. Maybe the way to convince her was...

He bent his head and touched his mouth to hers, brushed his lips across those curves, and pressed softly. She gave a small gasp and her taste flowed into him, a familiar honey. Twelve years of wanting clutched at his chest, his gut. Chris deepened the kiss, bringing up a hand to cup her shoulder.

And got a slap on the cheek that snapped his eyes wide open.

Chapter Four

A huge knot of *something*—Jayne decided to call it anger—
clogged her throat, preventing her from telling Chris Hammond what he could do with his kisses. So she jerked out of
his hold and strode back toward the library, hoping his cheek
hurt even half as much as her hand did after that slap.

Then she remembered the bruises and scrapes on his face
from the accident and felt guilty for making them worse.

But he had no business doing *that,* she argued with herself
as she put another log on the fire and then went to wrap up in
a blanket on the empty couch. She couldn't possibly have
signaled that she was interested in any kind of physical contact, because she definitely was not.

Although, a traitorous part of her whispered, *his mouth* was
delicious! He tasted of coffee, with a dark edge that owed
nothing to the brew she'd served. An exotic, enticing flavor
she'd never encountered in all her history of kisses. Not that she'd
kissed so many men. And most of them had been quite…safe.

Chris Hammond was anything but safe. He said he'd seen
the birthmark on her hip, had even kissed it. The intimacy
implied by such knowledge left her breathless. She refused
to name the emotion that left her pulse pounding.

As for the idea that the mark identified her as this Juliet Radcliffe…

Surely other women had birthmarks on their left hips. Jayne's grandmother had called hers a J, for their shared name. Or a fishing hook. The resemblance to Italy had never crossed Jayne's mind. But then, she'd never had a lover who kissed it, either.

She fell asleep trying to determine how she would behave with Chris Hammond in the morning, and how soon she could send him back to town. The school owned several vehicles with four-wheel drive, so if the snow wasn't too deep she would just lend him an SUV and ask him to leave it at the police station.

But when the first ray of sunlight wedged her lids apart, she doubted she'd be sending anyone anywhere for quite some time. Snow lay three feet deep, perhaps more, against the panes of the floor-to-ceiling French doors leading into the private garden. Beyond the surrounding stone wall lay a pure white carpet with no hint of shrubs, steps, driveway or landscape. At the edge of the surrounding forest, the branches of pine and cedar trees sagged under thick dollops of white frosting, and even the skeletons of the oaks and maples and beeches glistened with snow.

This morning, the phone did not work. They were completely snowed in until the weather warmed up or someone with a plow or a snowmobile came to get them. Jayne wasn't sure which would happen first.

As more sparkling sunlight entered the room, the girls on the floor began to stir. Rubbing her eyes, Taryn stumbled to the nearest window and glanced out at the scenery.

"Awesome," she cried. "Hey, guys, come look!"

In the next moment, they were all exclaiming over the snow.

"Cool!"

"I've never seen so much snow."

"Let's go outside!"

In unison they turned toward the door, but Jayne stood in their way. When she held up a hand, silence fell.

"Breakfast first," she told them. "Before breakfast, you need to fold your bedding neatly and put it with your pillows across the hall in the conference room so we don't have to step over them all day. Then you can go to your rooms to dress and bring back the jackets, hats, gloves and boots you'll need to go outside. Understood?"

The seven girls nodded solemnly. But as soon as they left the conference room, they reverted to extreme excitement, dancing along the hallway toward the stairs, talking loudly and making wild plans for all the fun to be had in the snow.

After putting a pot of water for instant oatmeal over some of the coals in the fireplace, Jayne went to her office to change. A long and exhausting day awaited her, without a doubt. After the novelty wore off, some girls would want to be inside, some out. Without music, television and movies, the girls would be looking to her for entertainment. The puzzles and games she'd bought wouldn't be nearly enough. She had not, Jayne was dismayed to admit, planned for this many girls. She hadn't planned for a blizzard.

And she certainly hadn't planned on Chris Hammond, who was stuck here just as surely as the rest of them for the foreseeable future.

"Good morning." He was leaning on the second-story rail as she entered the entry hall from the office wing. "Looks like we're snowed in."

"Good morning. Yes, I don't think there's much chance of driving out of here until the snow melts." The memory of last night's kiss flooded her mind, urging her to cut the conversation short.

Instead, though, she heard herself ask, "Did you sleep well?"

He started down the stairs. "Until a gaggle of girls stampeded past the infirmary a few minutes ago, screaming at the tops of their lungs."

Jayne couldn't make herself move until he reached the bottom step and joined her. "I'm insisting on breakfast first, so I'd better start cooking."

"Does that mean there's a chance of coffee?" Chris fell in step beside her.

"I'll see what I can do." She pushed open the door into the library wing and held it for him to come though after her. "You're pretty stiff this morning." Though why she should comment, let alone notice, was more than she could explain.

"I've felt worse."

"While you were working?"

"A couple of times."

"Taking pictures in the middle of a war seems foolhardy." Jayne spooned instant coffee into two mugs. "But I suppose we need to know what's going on."

"Truth and consequences." When she turned around, his gaze fixed immediately on her face. "Last night wasn't my first vehicle crash, either."

"Really?" She felt his eyes like pricks from a sword point as she walked into the library to ladle heated water into the mugs. "Does that mean you're not a good driver?"

"I was a kid, the first time around." He didn't stop watching her as he took a long drink. "But it was a slick mountain road, just like last night."

The long silence, and the pressure of his unswerving focus, broke Jayne's nerve.

"Why are you staring at me?" she demanded. "Is there a problem, Mr. Hammond?"

"Call me Chris, for God's sake." He clanked his mug down on the library table. "As for problems—here's the big one. I can't believe—"

Taryn burst into the kitchen, pigtails flying. "Is there breakfast yet? I'm starved!" She caught sight of Chris. "Did you see how much snow we got? Isn't it wild? I can't wait to start sledding."

Monique and Selena came in behind her, with the other girls on their heels, all of them nearly as excited as when they'd left to get dressed.

Thankful to have whatever he was about to say postponed, Jayne shifted her attention to food. "We've got oatmeal," she announced, "orange juice, bananas, apples, sugar and butter."

Haley flopped on the sofa. "I hate oatmeal."

"I usually eat half a bagel," Sarah added.

Jayne took a deep breath. "There is also cold cereal and milk, bagels and cream cheese."

"But no toaster," Monique pointed out.

"So toast over the fire," Chris suggested. "All you need is a long, pointed stick."

Jayne looked up at him from where she crouched by the fire. "There are toasting forks," she told him. "In the main kitchen behind the dining hall. We use them as decorations on the wall."

He gave her a two-fingered salute. "Be right back."

In his absence, Jayne marshaled the girls into the kitchen to set the table for breakfast. As she ladled water for those who wanted oatmeal, Chris supervised the toasting process and produced enough warm, buttered bread for all of them to enjoy. The cleanup process was another group effort, made more difficult by everyone's eagerness to enjoy the snow. Everyone but Jayne.

Finally, with the kitchen tidied to her satisfaction, she gave the girls permission to go outside. "Stay near this building," she told them from the front portico of the manor. "I'll expect to see all of you when I get out there."

She fetched her own boots, coat, hat and gloves from her office, and had her hand on the doorknob again when Chris joined her.

"You don't exactly look enthusiastic." He'd scavenged a bulky coat, wool cap and work gloves from the cleaning staff's office.

"I hate snow," she told him, opening the door to avoid being alone with him even for a moment. She didn't want to give him a chance to finish that sentence he'd started earlier.

"Why?" His voice was casual, and when she glanced at him, he was watching the girls rolling barrel-style down the hills on the Hawkridge lawn. "Did you grow up in Michigan, with snow every winter, shoveling day in and day out?"

She started to remind him of the accusations he'd already made about her background, but realized at the last moment that he'd laid a very neat trap for her to fall into.

Well, she would spring that trap, without getting caught. "I grew up about fifty miles from here, in the mountains. We had snow there, though rarely this much." She smiled when he frowned in her direction. "But I don't know why I don't enjoy it. I get cold very quickly. I worry about slipping and falling—I've got a slight weakness on my left side that makes me less stable if I'm not thinking." She shrugged. "I'd rather be sitting on a warm beach in the sunshine than feel ice crystals sliding down my back and into my shoes."

"You weren't locked out in the cold, or fall down a long hill? No getting lost in the snowy woods?"

Fear fluttered in Jayne's chest. "No. I don't remember anything like that." She wasn't about to confess to this nosy stranger how few memories she had to draw on.

"So why did you take a job in the mountains?"

Since coming to Hawkridge School, she'd asked herself that question every autumn and all winter long. "I wanted to do the work here. These troubled girls need the kind of help I've been trained to offer."

"They look fairly normal and happy to me."

Jayne couldn't help a chuckle as she surveyed the scene. Taryn and Haley were rolling down the hill, standing up at the bottom covered with huge chunks of snow. Then they climbed back up to do it again. Monique and Selena were making a large snowball, presumably the bottom of a snow person to pair with the one Sarah and Beth had already started. In a corner by herself, Yolanda was creating a host of snow angels.

"I've rarely seen all of them in a good mood at the same time," Jayne said, surprised.

But even as she said it, the spell of enchantment broke. Monique stomped away from Selena and the lopsided snowball they'd formed, trudging over to join Sarah and Beth, who didn't appear to welcome her intrusion. Halfway down the hill, Taryn collided with Haley, who sat up crying and rubbing her head.

"So much for peace on Earth," Chris muttered, as Jayne started down the steps.

Halfway down, she wobbled, just a little. Then her feet slipped out from under her.

Chris launched himself forward and managed to get his hands under her arms just before she fell. With a heave that left his shoulder screaming bloody murder, he hauled her up and back against him. For a few seconds he bore her full weight, and even through the layers of coats and clothes he could feel the curves of her body pressed into his.

Fuller, he thought. *Lush. Mature.* Juliet had been a girl when he last held her, still bony, a little awkward. Now, though, she was completely a woman.

Or else this wasn't Juliet at all.

He banished the traitorous thought as she straightened away from him. "Thanks," she said breathlessly, with a glance over her shoulder. "That would have hurt."

"No problem." Forcing his arms to loosen, he took a deep breath. "You need a handrail on these steps."

"The board of directors is at war with the local safety inspector on that very topic." She hesitated, staring at the steps below them. "Historical integrity versus legal issues. We do have ramps at other doors."

Taking her arm, Chris started down slowly, urging her to lean against him slightly. He expected resistance, but this time she gave in without a fight.

Once on the ground, though, she pulled free and side-stepped down the hill through the deep snow to kneel beside Haley, who was still crying.

"Are you hurt?" Jayne took off her gloves and wiped the girl's tear-streaked cheeks with her fingertips. "Can you stand up?"

With her lower lip stuck out, Haley shook her head.

"She's such a baby." Taryn stood to the side, arms crossed over her chest. "I barely touched her."

"She crashed into my head and ran over me." Despite her "injuries," Haley struggled to her feet. "On purpose."

"Did not. It was an accident." Taryn's voice rose in volume.

The headmistress shuffled through churned up snow to stand between them. "The two of you need to calm down."

Her words went unheeded. "You liar," Haley growled. "You said you were gonna roll over me like a bulldozer."

"I am not a liar." Before the words were finished, Taryn launched herself at Haley and took her down into the snow, wrestling, punching and kicking. In an instant the rest of the girls circled around, calling encouragement to their favorite. Arguments started between opposing fans, leading to shoving and yelling. Chris headed down to break up the fight.

The loudest whistle he'd ever heard brought him up short. Total silence followed, and total stillness. Even the wind stopped, and the birds stayed quiet as he and the girls stared at the source of that sound—Jayne Thomas herself.

She stared at each of her students in their turn. "Inside," she said, her voice stiff, cold, implacable. "Now."

Turning, she marched up the hill without looking back. A single line of girls followed in her footsteps, silently, without arguing, around the side of the manor to the door Chris had used last night to check the generator. Jayne held the door open and the girls filed in.

"Jackets, hats, boots and gloves in the storeroom," she ordered. "Then sit in the library, on the floor near the fire."

Chris came last, putting a hand on the door to allow her to go in ahead of him. "Quite a show of power, there. Why are they so afraid of you?"

"Don't I look scary?" She huffed a laugh as she pulled off her green wool cap, and her ponytail came loose with it. Mahogany curls fell over her shoulders and across her eyes. Pushing the hair off her face, she frowned. "Maybe I do right now. But they're not afraid of *me*. Hawkridge is their last chance and they know it. They either graduate or go to jail."

Chris fisted his hands against the urge to help smooth her messy, shining hair. "I guess that's not a hard choice."

"More so for some than others." Still combing her fingers through the tangles, she marched toward the storeroom doorway. "Come on, girls. You don't want this to take all day."

Chris stayed in the hallway for the next twenty minutes, leaning against the wall and listening to the proceedings without interrupting. Jayne delivered her lecture in a crisp voice unlike the soft drawl he'd heard so far. She talked about responsibility, self-discipline and respect for others and self, following up with expectations, goals and consequences. By the end, Chris was examining his own conscience—a rare event.

Since first recognizing Jayne Thomas as Juliet Radcliffe, down in Ridgeville, he'd been obsessed with finding out why she'd disappeared, leaving him all these years to think she was dead. He hadn't cared if he scared her, showing up unannounced at the school. And he'd bullied her, or tried to—she was hard to intimidate. Chris had wanted the truth and was prepared to do whatever might be required.

Did he have the truth yet? Nothing he'd done or said so far had convinced Jayne to admit her story about growing up with her grandmother in a town across the mountains was just that—fiction. He could almost believe she didn't remember anything at all about Ridgeville, or about him.

So which option was worse? That she didn't remember their time together? That she didn't want to acknowledge a relationship with him? Or that she'd died on that long ago Christmas Eve?

Chris was beginning to think he'd hurt less if he could go on believing Juliet was dead. The old pain was almost comfortable, compared to the idea that Juliet didn't want him in her life. And how in the world could she simply forget their time together? Their love?

She hadn't forgotten; she'd put a whole set of childhood

memories in place of the ones they'd made together. Her family's house fire, for example. Where had that idea come from? Why make that choice? Why fabricate a childhood at all?

Inside the library, Jayne issued instructions for a quiet morning—books, puzzles, solitary card games. After lunch, they'd all go out to the snow bowl, as she'd promised, if—*if*, she repeated—peace reigned through lunch.

Chris straightened up from the wall, having modified his own plan for the remainder of his time at Hawkridge. Maybe Juliet didn't want him in her life. If so, she was going to have to explain why. Maybe she didn't remember him and Ridgeville. Maybe she'd forgotten everything between them. If so, he wanted to know what had happened to her memory. Either way, there was a mystery here begging for an explanation. As a journalist committed to probing for the truth, Chris could never let a mystery go unsolved.

And if Jayne Thomas turned out to be just who she claimed?

Well, then Juliet would be dead. And he'd live with the guilt, as he had been for the last twelve years.

But he would coax a real smile onto Jayne Thomas's full lips before he moved on.

AFTER MODERATING a discussion among the girls on anger management techniques, Jayne decreed a quiet time for individual activities during the ninety minutes before lunch. Reading, solo work on puzzles and games, even napping were acceptable activities. Communication of any kind was not. They needed the peace as much as she did.

Chris Hammond had vanished when she looked for him out in the hallway, which was just as well. She didn't want to interact with him, didn't want to be reminded of that kiss by the doors last night, or those moments this morning when he held her against him, his arms firm around her, his body like a tree trunk against which she could take shelter from the storm. She'd felt safe and cared for, guarded by his strength.

Worst of all, his embrace, his body, had felt as familiar as her own. He smelled like…like *home*. And his taste—that blend of coffee with something deep and dark and intoxicating—hadn't surprised her at all.

He felt, smelled, tasted familiar. *Damn it.*

"Ms. Thomas?"

Jayne looked up from her mug of coffee and the book she'd pretended to read. "Yes, Taryn?"

The girl stood beside her chair, twisting a strand of hair around her finger. "I'm hungry. When is lunch?"

A glance at her watch showed that her ninety minutes of calm had almost ended. "As soon as we get it ready." Once on her feet, she looked around the library at the girls in their various locations. "Let's set up a sandwich bar," she announced, "and everyone can make their own sub, exactly the way they want it."

Harmony reigned during the preparations, since no one wanted to spend the afternoon in isolation. Monique volunteered to slice tomatoes and even onions, at Haley's request, while Selena spooned ice into cups for soft drinks. In less than fifteen minutes, the kitchen counter was transformed into a delicatessen offering a wide selection of sandwich options.

"Line up alphabetically by last name," Jayne told the girls. "Lunch is served!"

She rethought her instructions when she realized that alphabetical order put Haley Farrish at the head of the line with Taryn Gage right behind her. But the girls assembled their lunches side by side without incident.

Just to remind Jayne not to relax her guard, Yolanda began to complain. "Why am I always last?"

Jayne stepped in behind her. "Now you're not last. I am."

Yolanda rolled her eyes. "Yeah, but I still have to eat stuff that's been picked over and everybody else has put their dirty fingers on."

"That's why we have spoons," Sarah pointed out. "And why we wash our hands before we eat."

"Blah, blah, blah," Yolanda said. "Talk all you want. I know what I see."

Taryn turned around to glare at the older girl. "Why don't you just—"

"What?" Yolanda stepped closer to the seventh grader. "What do you want me to do?"

When Taryn caught sight of Jayne's warning look and the firm shake of her head, she settled for a superior sneer. "Never mind."

Lunch passed quietly after that, lacking conflict but also lacking the laughter that usually enlivened time with the girls. Lacking, as well, the challenge of dealing with Chris Hammond.

"Where'd Mr. Hammond go?" Haley looked around the kitchen, as if he were hiding somewhere, waiting to be discovered. "Doesn't he want lunch?"

"I don't know," Jayne was forced to reply. "He came inside with us."

"I saw him through the window a few minutes ago," Selena volunteered. "He was walking down the driveway."

Jayne fought to keep her face blank. Without comment, she returned to her sandwich.

Had he decided to leave? Without telling her or…or anyone? No one with intelligence would try to walk all the way to Ridgeville in three feet of snow. And expecting to find a ride on the road was a ridiculous idea. The plows wouldn't reach this area for several days.

Of course, she didn't really know him, so she couldn't

decide what he might choose to do. Maybe he wasn't as smart as she'd thought.

As the girls cleaned up the kitchen, Jayne finished her coffee and tried to talk herself out of the unreasonable dismay she felt at Chris Hammond's departure. He complicated her life, distracting her from the students for whom she was responsible. His absurd obsession with her "false" identity made him unpredictable and unreliable. She should be glad he'd left—that meant he'd decided to believe the truth and stop pestering her.

She *was* glad he'd left. Her single-handed custody of these seven girls could now proceed without interference.

With their chores done, they had gathered around her in an attitude of expectation. "Can we go to the snow bowl now, Ms. Thomas? Can we?"

"Yes. Get dressed and we'll hike up there."

With the situation restored to normal, all of them prepared to go back outside. Bundled up once more, they headed down the hallway toward the side exit as a group, the students chattering and giggling, Jayne pulling on her gloves and tugging her hat down over her ears.

Just as Yolanda reached for the door handle, the panel swung away from her, pulled outward by an unseen hand. Several of the girls squealed in shock or fright. Jayne jumped, and her heart started racing.

Chris Hammond stood just outside the door, holding his hat in one hand. Powdered with snow from shoulders to toes, his hair wet and tousled, he looked as if he'd fought through an avalanche to reach them. Excitement snapped and crackled in his blue eyes.

He winked at Yolanda, now staring at him with her mouth open, nodded at Jayne, and then grinned at the entire group.

"Who's up for an afternoon snowball fight?"

Chapter Five

"I hate snow." Jayne muttered the words to herself over and over that afternoon as she watched from the lip of the round, shallow valley, which the blizzard had coated with white icing. On one slope, four or five girls whirled down the walls of the bowl on blue disks. Snow people in various stages of construction stood sentry along the edges.

And at the center stood Chris Hammond, defending himself against snowballs thrown from all directions. He had hiked across campus, he'd explained, as far as the school gymnasium, where he'd pulled out the sleds and snowshoes stored in the equipment room.

The building was locked, he'd said in answer to Jayne's query, but he'd had the foresight to take with him the ring of keys hanging in the maintenance office in the manor. As she stared at him, appalled, he'd reassured her that he'd left the building as secure as he found it. Then he gave her that heart-stopping grin.

Now he constituted the center of battle. Girls joined the fight at different times, stayed for a while and then drifted off to some other game, only to return later and renew their attack. His dramatic reactions to hits, misses and his own missiles—lobbed rather than thrown, Jayne was certain—

kept everyone laughing. He had made their afternoon at The Nest a special event.

She wanted to laugh, to be entertained. But her feet were cold inside her fleece-lined boots, and she was sure her nose was red. Her hands were warm enough, thanks to thick sheepskin gloves and the wool coat pockets she'd tucked them into. But she was tired of standing and watching. As for joining in…not an option.

Though she willed the time to pass more quickly, the sun clung stubbornly to the tops of the trees and the glare reflecting off the snow seared her eyes. She squeezed her lids together, letting darkness soothe the aching tissues.

Even with her eyes closed, she saw snow. In her mind's eye, the night sky hung over her and the wind lashed her face when branches didn't. Black tree trunks barred her way on every side. She stumbled….

Opening her eyes, Jayne shook her head. What was *that?* A scene from a movie? Or another winter, when she'd taken a walk at night in the snow…something she couldn't remember ever having done?

No matter how hard she tried, she couldn't find the smallest scrap of a memory like the vision she'd just witnessed. As often happened when she tried to recall the past, she came up against a solid blank wall. No faces, no places, no events reached her from the other side. She couldn't climb over the wall, dig under or go around.

Tears blurred her vision, and she reluctantly dragged her hands out of her pockets so she could wipe her eyes. As her sight cleared, she saw a lone figure climbing the slope in her direction.

"I lost," Chris announced as he joined her on the rim. "Beaten by a bunch of girls. Good thing no one's here as a witness."

"Ahem. No one?"

Still grinning, he raised his eyebrows. "Would you rat out an old friend?"

"Two days doesn't make us old friends."

"Oh, yeah. I forgot—we didn't know each other before." He clicked his tongue. The grin had vanished. "It's hard to ignore these pictures in my mind, though. I see you naked, asleep on a blanket in the grass just after we've made love. Pretty unforgettable."

Fear exploded in Jayne's stomach and roiled into her chest. She closed her fingers into fists. "I don't doubt you had that experience. I'm sure you remember someone. I," she said carefully, holding his gaze, "am not she."

"Another denial. With perfect grammar, no less." Chris noticed the sudden flush on the headmistress's cheeks, the speedup of her puffs of breath in the frigid air. "Then what are you so afraid of?"

Instead of answering, she stomped to the edge of the ridge. The whistle she gave was a repeat of this morning's—loud, long and piercing, bringing the whole world, including the girls, to a complete stop.

"Time to go," she shouted, her hands cupped around her mouth. Then she raised her arms and motioned for them to come.

After the long afternoon spent playing in the cold, the lack of protest from the girls wasn't a surprise. They had to be tired. Chris knew he was exhausted and freezing. The sun dropped suddenly behind the trees, and the temperature plunged with it.

But the level of whining on the hike back to the school shocked and irritated him.

"My toes hurt." That was Haley's complaint. During the fight this afternoon he'd managed to learn all their names.

Beth grumbled, "I'm hungry." Since Jayne had, with foresight, insisted on bringing water and plenty of trail mix for snacks, Chris couldn't understand how anyone could be hungry.

Even sunny Selena voiced a complaint. "These boots are too small."

"Walk slower. I can't keep up." As the smallest, Taryn always seemed to be lagging behind.

"This is taking forever." Monique had long legs and the long stride to match. "Can't we go faster?"

Chris set his jaw, keeping his teeth clenched against the urge to answer. Feeling Jayne's glance, he looked over and caught her quizzical look.

"That's how most kids behave at the end of the day. Don't hold it against them."

Yolanda piped up from behind him. "How much longer do we have to walk?"

Ever helpful Sarah added, "Are you sure we're not lost?" A chorus of gasps greeted the suggestion.

Jayne stopped and turned to face them. "No, we are not lost. We're following our own footsteps on the path out of the woods. We've got another ten minutes to walk before we reach the lawn.

"You all are making a bad impression on Mr. Hammond." She looked at each of the girls directly. "He doesn't know what to do with a bunch of brats who only have to walk back to a reasonable shelter for the night after a day of nothing but play. Think about it."

Their last ten minutes passed in silence, though the girls seemed more thoughtful than mad.

When they finally came out of the woods, though, another chorus of gasps met the sight of the manor standing in the twilight like a snow-covered castle in a fairy tale…without a single glimmer of light anywhere.

The headmistress stopped in her tracks.

"Not exactly the homecoming you expected," Chris muttered.

"Um, no. I'd forgotten for a moment." She started hiking again, with more energy, and they were far enough ahead of the girls that her hesitation didn't register with anyone but him. "Once we get inside and light the fire, we'll all be fine." She glanced back at the girls. "I think."

Even with the nine of them gathered around the hearth and the fire snapping sharply, the mood remained sober. No giggling, no teasing or squabbling—there was none of the teenage noise Chris had gotten used to in the last twenty-four hours. These teenagers seemed more like children tonight, for some reason. Lonely children.

Jayne stepped inside the library door. "This morning, I took Mrs. Rosen's stew out of the freezer to thaw. We'll heat it up in pot on the fire, so dinner won't take much work or time.

"In fact," she said more gently, looking at the huddle in front of the fire, "I'll get out the bowls and the bread so all of you can stay here and warm up." She went back to the kitchen without meeting Chris's eyes.

He couldn't let the sadness continue. "Where was I?"

Taryn wrinkled her forehead as she looked at him. "Huh?"

"Chase and Juliet. I was telling you about them."

A couple of the other girls perked up. "There's more?" Selena asked.

"Oh, yeah. I told you the end of the story, remember? He killed her. Would you like to know why?"

"Did she screw somebody else?"

"Whoa." Chris stared at Yolanda, the source of the question. "They're just thirteen years old at this point."

She shrugged. "So?"

"So they're kids. Nobody's screwing anybody."

Yolanda shrugged. "They are in my neighborhood."

"This isn't your neighborhood," Selena told her. Then she turned back to Chris. "Okay, so he took her to his granddad's house. Then what happened?"

Relieved to be finished with the tricky stuff, Chris stirred the fire, arranging a bed of coals underneath the pot stand just as Jayne came in carrying her huge kettle of stew.

"What did Juliet see when she went into Chase's grandfather's house?"

Chris winked at Sarah in thanks for her leading question. "The inside of Charlie's house—that's Chase's granddad, remember—reminded Juliet of a magic store."

Charlie was an inventor and a science teacher. He liked to experiment, and his "projects," as he called them, occupied the nooks and crannies, the tables and shelves and counters in every room of his rambling old cabin. Flasks of bubbling liquids hung over low fires, while beakers of bright metallic liquids and squares of colorful powders sat within reach. The house smelled like wood ash and spiced apples and rust—the apples were part of dinner that night, but who knew what else might be cooking?

For the next week, Juliet showed up at Charlie's every day, on a bicycle she said she'd found in her grandmother's garage. She and Chase watched Charlie experiment, played in the snow that finally fell on Christmas Eve, and sledded down the hill in back of the cabin on trash-can lids.

Being with Juliet was like having a favorite sister, Chase decided. Even if some of his thoughts weren't brotherly at all.

The night before she was scheduled to leave for New York, Charlie fed the two kids ham and carrots from his own garden sweetened with honey from his beehive, along with apples from the trees in his backyard. Then he showed them a few tricks—how coiled electric wire could become a magnet, how purple iodine crystals, dropped into a colorless liquid, disappeared, and how two clear liquids, when combined, produced a beautiful yellow powder. Chase exhibited his granddad's collection of crystals and geodes. For once, Juliet wasn't bored. She'd never had so much fun.

Then Charlie said, "I reckon you'd better get home, young lady. It's dark and nobody knows where you are."

"They probably haven't noticed I'm gone." Juliet sighed. "They were having a party this afternoon. Everybody's drunk by now."

Drunk or not, Juliet's family had called the police when they found her gone after sunset. When Charlie stopped his 1952 Chevy at the end of a long, winding driveway, red and blue lights flashed in front of the chalet-style mansion Juliet claimed was her grandmother's home.

"You're in a pile of trouble, young lady."

"So what's new?" She leaned forward from the backseat. "I'll walk from here so you don't get involved."

"I don't think so—" Charlie began, but Juliet was out of the car before he could turn around. Chase opened his own door, ready to go after her, but she vanished before he got both feet on the ground.

"She went into the trees on the right," Charlie said. "You'll never find her."

Chase dropped back into the Chevy. "Will she be all right?"

"I hope so." His granddad shifted gears and backed out onto the road. "She's an awful cute little gal."

Chris stayed quiet for a minute, and the girls gradually realized that he'd finished.

"Wait," Selena said, sitting up. "You can't stop there. What happened to Juliet?"

"How does Chase see her again?"

"Did her folks let her see him?"

Chris looked at Jayne and found her as absorbed as the girls, absentmindedly stirring the pot while she listened to him with her chin propped on one hand.

"I thought you all might want some supper. Looks to me like Ms. Thomas has your stew ready to eat," he said.

She blinked hard and sat up straight. "Exactly. We're ready for dinner."

Yolanda stopped in front of him on her way to the kitchen. "But you'll tell more later tonight?" Her gaze was fierce, but anxious, too.

Chris nodded. "I can do that."

ONCE THE GIRLS WERE READY for bed, Chris picked up the story where he'd left off.

Chase tried not to mope during the rest of his vacation with Charlie, but he couldn't think of anything fun to do by himself. He hung around town, hoping maybe Juliet had stayed longer and would show up again to steal a candy bar. He rode his bike out to the expensive new housing development where he and Charlie had dropped her off that night, and looked at the chalet in the daylight. When he coasted farther down the driveway, he saw that a tall iron gate blocked the drive, with a fence stretching into the trees on either side. There were dogs behind the fence, German shepherds who made a lot of noise. Maybe Juliet knew them and could get past them, but Chase had the feeling he'd regret climbing over.

So he celebrated the New Year with Charlie until he had to get on a plane in Asheville and fly back to Philly. Then there was school—long, gray, boring days of school, which were only better compared to the…

Chris hesitated over his word choice. He should back off a little on the intensity. "—compared to the war of words he walked into every night at home."

As he looked at the girls, he saw Beth nodding her head. "I know how that goes," she said softly.

"You and me both," Yolanda agreed.

"Chase didn't forget Juliet, but the days passed and he went with the flow, especially once baseball season started. Guys," he said with an apologetic shrug, "like sports."

"Yeah, yeah." Monique sniffed. "So then what?"

"So then the school year ended. Chase's mother was spending the summer in Europe and his dad would be working in Egypt, so they sent Chase to live with Charlie for the entire summer vacation."

Nothing could have suited Chase better. He loved the mountains, liked helping Charlie around the yard and in the garden, and enjoyed watching him work on his experiments. The stress of the months at home fell away—he gained weight, slept through the nights and woke up looking forward to his day.

There were times Charlie got so wrapped up in a project he forgot he had a grandson, and so Chase started exploring the mountains around the cabin, most of which formed parts of several different national parks. As long as he returned for dinner, Charlie didn't bother about where he might have spent the day.

Or who he spent it with, which was good because Juliet was back. Chase stopped by the market in town to pick up lunch supplies for the day and was trying to decide between plain chips and barbecued when someone tapped him on the shoulder.

"Boo," she said into his ear.

Chase jerked around, only to drop the bag of cookies, three cans of soda, four candy bars and two sub sandwiches he'd been holding because he'd forgotten to get a basket.

"Such a geek," Beth groaned, with her hand over her face.

"I think he's cute," Haley said.

"So did Juliet," Chris told them.

She squatted down with him to help pick up the food.

"I'm here for the summer," she said, standing up with the chips in one hand and a drink in the other. "My folks wanted me out of the city, away from my friends because they're a bad influence." Her tone was mocking. "Can you believe it?"

Clutching sandwiches, drinks and candy, Chase stared at her and believed it. Juliet had bleached her hair to a dry wheat color, cut it short and spiked it in all directions. Black makeup circles rimmed her eyes. Metal spikes on chains hung in her ears. She wore a tight black T-shirt, baggy black pants with chains hanging from the pockets, and black military boots.

He gulped. "Hi."

Turning toward the checkout lanes, she grabbed another bag of chips from the shelf as she talked to him over her shoulder. "You can't tell Charlie I'm here, though. My grandmother knows who he is and my folks told her to make sure I didn't see him or you ever again."

"Why?" Chase paid for the supplies and grabbed the grocery bag, following Juliet outside.

"Because you kidnapped me at Christmas, of course."

"Kidnapped you?" Who was this person? What had happened to the girl he'd met over the holidays?

She dropped onto the bench they'd occupied before. "Why else would I have disappeared?"

"Did you tell them we'd kidnapped you?"

"Not exactly." Opening the chip bag, she avoided his eyes. "I just said you'd taken me to your house and kept me there, and that's why I wasn't at home when they looked for me."

Chase muttered a swear word Charlie would have smacked him for. "They might have arrested us. They still could!"

"No, they won't. I promised to let them know where I was at all times."

"Like now? They know you're in town?"

"Yes. I told them I was going to the library."

"Oh." Chase considered the prospect of spending the day inside with a book. Not possible. "Okay, well—"

Juliet hopped to her feet. "So where are we really going?"

That was when he knew she hadn't changed at all.

AFTER SPENDING HALF the day outdoors in the cold, none of the girls stayed awake long enough to hear the end of the night's installment. Jayne had heard all the words, but was so drowsy she couldn't have said what they meant. With her eyes half-open, she saw Chris put more logs on the fire and arrange the blaze for a nice, even burn. He turned toward her and seemed to stare at her for a long time, but that could have been her dreamy state of mind. At last his flashlight beam cut the shadows, then wandered into the hallway. He'd left his wet boots and socks by the outside door, so she couldn't hear his footsteps.

She'd spent quite a bit of time this evening trying not to stare at his strong, well-built feet.

Sinking into sleep, Jayne found herself riding a bicycle up and down long, smooth hills. In the dream, she wasn't even surprised to be on a bicycle; she recalled the story she'd been listening to and recognized the power of suggestion. Anyway, she was enjoying the ride, the wind in her face and the sense of physical effort without getting tired in the least.

The sensation of a threat came over her all at once, an awareness that she had to ride faster to escape something—someone?—dire. Breathing hard, she tried to increase her speed, but knew without a doubt she was losing ground. Underneath her weight, the bike wobbled and shook. Pieces started popping off and clattering to the asphalt roadway. Hot, moist breath seared the back of her neck. A hand gripped her shoulder just as the bicycle disintegrated. She jerked away and fell, with rocks tearing her skin as she slid across the pavement, then slammed to a stop. Struggling and sobbing, she sat up against the tree trunk, which became a wall at her back. And when she looked up, he was there—

Jayne gasped and woke up, halfway to her feet before she even realized her eyes were open.

In front of her, the fire in the hearth flickered gently, casting gold shadows on the sleeping girls spread across the carpet. At the windows, icy moonlight polished silver snow.

She took a few deep breaths, getting her bearings, then stepped carefully over arms and legs and feet on her way to the library door. A glass of juice, or even water, would help her settle down and go back to sleep.

Sitting at the kitchen table in the dark, she tried and failed to forget the dream. The symbolism wasn't hard to decipher—Chris Hammond's story, the accident that landed him at Hawkridge, even the menace she felt following her could be related to him.

The danger in her dream, however, hadn't felt connected to the bike ride. It…no, *he* had come from outside, from elsewhere. And she didn't know who he could be or why she had been so scared.

"Can't sleep?"

Jayne jumped and sloshed orange juice on the table. "I didn't hear you coming."

Chris Hammond took a glass from the cabinet, poured himself some milk and came to sit across from her at the table. "Me, neither." That was, she supposed, the reply to his question and her comment.

He didn't turn on a flashlight, but they didn't need one. Moonlight reflected off snow poured through the window, brighter than electric lamps.

Even so, electricity filled the silence. Jayne tried a casual comment to diffuse the tension. "You must be tired, after playing in the snow all afternoon. On top of your accident."

He rolled that left shoulder in backward circles, drawing her attention to the muscles underneath his sky-blue sweater. "The exercise was good—kept the ligaments and tendons from getting stiff."

"If you say so." She sounded like a prude, even to herself. "I think warm milk is supposed to help you sleep. I don't know if cold works as well."

"A full stomach is all I need, besides getting my brain to turn off. That's the real problem. I can't stop thinking."

Despite the promptings of reason and common sense, she asked, "What are you thinking about?"

Propping his folded arms on the table, he leaned toward her. "Well, you see, I've come up with a plan that could prove or disprove your identity as Juliet Radcliffe."

"I've already told you—"

"But you're not an objective source."

"And you are?"

"No. But if we both agreed—either you are or you aren't—then the issue would be settled."

"And just how do you intend to provoke that agreement?"

He didn't move, but the intensity of his gaze on her face made her feel as if he'd gotten very close. "A good word choice, 'provoke.' My suggestion is this—let me spend thirty minutes seducing you."

Jayne slapped her hands on the table. "What?"

"Or you can seduce me, if that works better for you." He shrugged. "Either way, I think by the end of thirty minutes, we'll know for sure whether or not you are my Juliet."

Chapter Six

Jayne laughed at him. "You're not serious."

He responded with a frown, and gradually her amusement died. "That's ridiculous. Insane. Depraved," she added, when he didn't reply.

His eyes remained locked with hers, as if he could see the chaos of fear and excitement and desire churning her blood. Jayne broke the connection herself, got up from the chair and went to the window. Perhaps staring out at the frozen landscape would cool her down.

"I don't think so." She cleared her throat. "No."

Chris came to stand beside her. "Why not?"

"Because there's no reason to expect that…that approach would…work." He was too close, too overwhelming. But she wouldn't give him the satisfaction of her retreat. "I'm already certain of the outcome. I don't need any…any proof."

Now he chuckled. "Another interesting word. And I do need…proof." His voice reminded her of a lion's purr.

If he kept staring at her, she was just going to fall into him. Maybe he was right. Maybe she was—

He straightened up. "I've never forced a woman yet, and I don't intend to start now." On his way out, he stopped at the table to down the rest of his milk. "Good night."

Let him go. Let him go. Let him go.

"On the other hand—" Jayne said, just as he reached the doorway.

Looking back at her over his shoulder, he lifted an eyebrow. "Yes?"

She took a step, then another. "It's possible…"

He turned to face her, arms folded over his chest. "Yes?"

"I mean, I know who I am, but maybe you would be convinced if we…if I *gave* you…proof."

"Does that mean yes?" Somehow he moved to stand in front of her, looking down, his arms loose at his sides. Not relaxed, though. Neither of them was relaxed.

"Not…not thirty minutes. I don't really think that's necessary. Do you?"

"I guess we'll find out."

His hands rose to cup her face, with his thumbs meeting at the point of her chin, his palms warm against her neck and his fingers spread over the back of her skull.

Like a chalice, she thought. *A goblet of precious wine.*

As she gazed into his face, he brought his mouth to hers and sipped at her lower lip, pulling gently until he barely touched the smooth inner flesh. A soft release, and then the same tasting of her upper lip, while her breathing quickened and her hands trembled. If he didn't take a real, full, hard kiss soon, she would puddle at his feet.

And maybe he understood what she was thinking, or maybe that was his breathing she heard, like a man who had run a long, hard race. His hands didn't move, but the kiss was there, all at once, the full press of his mouth on hers, the nip of his teeth behind those sensual, mobile lips. She wanted to cry with the beauty of being wanted. She wanted to feel this way forever.

And so she took hold of him, grabbed at his shoulders and

then wrapped her arms around his waist while he drank and drank from her mouth and she gave as much as he asked because she was filled, too. He took the one step required to layer her body under his, against the wall. His knee stayed right where he'd put it, so when his hands slid down her shoulder blades and her ribs and her spine, when he gripped her hips and pulled her tighter against him, the bulk of his thigh between hers was the sweetest force she'd ever known.

Without thought, she slipped her hands under the hem of his sweater, working her fingers over the rough waistband of his jeans to the glory of the smooth bare skin above. Breathless, she stroked up the incline of his back to those rawboned shoulders strung with lean, tense muscle.

His hands had wandered, as well, but with less success. "You have too many damn clothes on," he growled, fumbling with sweater and shirt and slacks, while his mouth explored the arch of her neck, the curl of her ear, the angle of her jaw. "I can't find you."

But then his fingers seared her ribs, and she gasped.

"That's better." In a single rough motion he pushed the barrier of her bra up and away. His palms claimed her breasts and her knees buckled, leaving her held upright by the wall and the roll of his hips and his leg pushed hard against her.

The roughness didn't matter. The lack of dignity, the desertion of principle and responsibility didn't bother Jayne at all. She wanted this, as she had never wanted anything in her life. If he chose to take her against the wall, or lying on the cold, hard floor, she would let him. The pleasure would be worth any price she had to pay.

Her wandering hands found the loose waist of his jeans again, and dipped beneath. Chris jerked his head up with a quick breath, then groaned.

But in the next moment, he set his mouth against her temple and murmured, "Take it easy." His body shifted and he withdrew his leg, allowing the fire between them to cool from flame to flicker. Rather than driving her to the next level, Chris was backing off. His hands slid to her sides, then to her hips, with her clothes again separating skin from skin. He didn't actively take her hands off him, underneath the jeans. But she understood he expected it, and so she did.

Jayne couldn't look at him, not after giving him so much power over her body. Leaning against the wall, she hoped her own legs would hold her upright. How embarrassing, to fall at his feet.

Dignity was back, she gathered. No doubt principle and responsibility would return in a moment.

She waited to speak until her voice would function and her lips could shape words. The tone was simply beyond her control. "Did you learn what you wanted to know?"

"I think so."

She felt his gaze, and finally found the courage to meet it. The despair in his face caught her by surprise.

But she'd already given him more than she could afford. She wouldn't give him her concern, as well. "So now we know."

With every ounce of willpower she possessed, she managed to step around him and walk a straight line across the kitchen to the doorway. "Let's make that the end of it."

Then she walked across the hall into the women's bathroom, where she ran water into the sink while she sat on the floor in the dark and cried.

CHRIS DISCOVERED THAT getting to sleep wasn't any easier after making love with Jayne…Juliet…the woman who'd melted so sweetly in his arms, than before. He might as well go roll around in the snow buck naked. That might cool his body off.

And he couldn't even say he now knew the answer. He'd been sincere when he thought a few minutes of necking would reveal whether this was his Juliet or not. For twelve years he'd lived on memories—every kiss, every moment they'd spent learning and enjoying each other's bodies. His palms still knew the arch of her ribs, the curves of her calves, the soft pillow of her breasts.

So how could he explain the differences, except to say that Jayne and Juliet were different women? Jayne's hips were round, her bottom heart-shaped and firm, compared to Juliet's slender form. Bony form, if the truth were told—though, of course, he never had. Would she have matured into this vo-luptuous woman, or retained her coltish figure?

Had those small, fragile breasts become firm and full? Once, he could count every bone in her spine. Had they been overlayed with flesh rounded perfectly to fit the curve of a man's fingers?

Chris wanted to say no. Though he might look like a fool, he could hardly believe that these changes would have over-taken Juliet in the twelve years they'd been apart. Nature didn't stray that far from the original pattern. Jayne Thomas and Juliet Radcliffe could be two different women.

But…her taste. He had kissed enough women in the years since to know that each possessed a unique flavor. Regardless of the meal, a recent drink or breath mints and chewing gum, every woman's mouth was as different as she was from all others.

Jayne and Juliet tasted exactly the same. Like a Golden De-licious apple eaten from the tree on a sunny morning. Like mountain water pouring down granite rock, like the scent of pine trees and summer rain. Every good and decent moment of his life was contained in that flavor.

Jayne and Juliet were the same woman. He had no doubt.

The only reasonable explanation for Jayne's lack of memory was amnesia. She had supplanted her missing memories with the grandmother, the house fire and whatever other details she imagined. He'd hoped recounting their past would bring back the truth she'd forgotten, but nothing had surfaced so far.

He would have to push her harder, with details she probably wouldn't want revealed to the girls. At the same time, he would have to undermine the memories she did have, quizzing her about all the specifics she would recall if that actually was her life.

After tossing and turning on the hard, narrow mattress for what seemed like hours, Chris groaned and levered himself off the bed. With a blanket folded around his shoulders, he went to stare out the window at the snow. He was planning an assault on the structure of Jayne's life without any kind of professional backup or advice. Was he risking her emotional health? Her sanity? Was the truth worth that much?

He wanted to find Juliet. Under these circumstances, would she want to be found?

Leaning his forehead against the cold glass, Chris closed his eyes.

God help him, he didn't know the answer to that question.

IN KEEPING WITH HER OWN frame of mind, breakfast on the second morning of the blizzard started out grouchy. Jayne allowed the girls to sleep an extra hour, but even the early risers grumbled when she roused them. Excitement always ruled the first snow day. The second, when sore muscles and fatigue took over, usually came as a disappointment.

She didn't suggest going outside and wasn't surprised when none of the girls did, either. A morning of indoor activities might restore their good spirits and energy for an afternoon out in the cold.

Chris came into the kitchen after everyone else had started on their cereal and toast. Jayne could only hope her face wasn't turning as dark red as her hair.

"We have oatmeal," she told him, avoiding eye contact. "Or cold cereal, or toast. Pretty much the same as yesterday."

"Warm sounds good." He heaped oatmeal, brown sugar and milk into his bowl, then took his usual place at the head of the table. "So, I was wondering when you start decorating for Christmas around this place."

A couple of girls audibly caught their breath, and all seven looked up from their breakfasts to stare at him. Jayne pulled in a deep breath of her own.

"We don't really celebrate, um, Christmas," she said, keeping her voice even. "It's just too complicated."

Chris raised both eyebrows over wide blue eyes. "Too complicated? What the he—"

She sent him a warning look.

He stopped and cleared his throat. "What does that mean?"

"I'm Jewish," Beth volunteered around a bite of bagel with cream cheese. "My family does Hanukkah."

"I'm a pagan." Taryn lifted her chin and crossed her arms over her chest. "I worship the Goddess and celebrate Yule."

"Well, I want Christmas." Selena clanked her mug on the table. "Just because I had to stay here doesn't mean I don't want to celebrate."

"Me, too." Monique never seemed to have a problem expressing her opinion. "I've been wondering where the decorations were. And I want some Christmas cookies. The sugar kind, with red and green icing."

Yolanda put up her hands, signaling halt. "If you start putting up all that shepherds and babies and angel stuff, I'm staying in my room, I don't care how cold it is. I won't sit around with that Nativity crap."

On Yolanda's right, Selena jerked around to stare at her friend. "Don't be so disrespectful. You're talking about Jesus and Mary."

"I'm talking about a bunch of—"

Jayne's whistle brought the argument to a halt. "Calm down, all of you. I don't want to hear another word until I ask someone to speak."

She didn't mention specific names, but as her gaze connected with Chris's, she conveyed the message that her instructions included him, too.

After sixty full seconds of silence, she looked at the girls around the table, then at Chris. "As I said, it's complicated. I don't want anyone retreating to their room when we have no heat. I don't like hurt feelings and outraged beliefs. So we don't celebrate any of the December holidays, other than the dinner we have marking the end of the first term and the beginning of winter vacation. In the past, we have sometimes had a party to welcome the New Year."

Selena opened her mouth to protest, but only a squeak emerged when Jayne shook her head.

"The kitchen needs to be cleaned up. Afterward, you should dress for a morning indoors. This afternoon you can play in the snow on campus. Any questions?"

Selena raised her hand. "But what about Christmas? It's as wrong to prevent me from celebrating as it is to force someone else to join in. I want some Christmas."

Monique said, "Me, too." Haley nodded in vigorous agreement.

Jayne acknowledged Sarah's request to speak. "I agree with Selena," the senior said in her gentle tone. "I've loved my years at Hawkridge, but I do miss how we used to decorate for the holidays. We still make a big deal out of Halloween, and May Day. But New Year's Eve isn't the same as Christmas."

"Yeah."

"That's right."

"But—"

Jayne sighed, and they quieted down. She thought for a moment, then said, "I don't know an answer that will satisfy everyone. So I'm turning the problem over to the people most affected…the seven of you. Perhaps you all can work out a solution to this dilemma. Let me know what you decide."

She gave them a single nod and left the kitchen. No noise followed her, no argument or protest or complaint.

Nothing but one troublesome male. Chris caught up with her as she walked down the hall. "Interesting maneuver you came up with."

"A maneuver that wouldn't have been necessary if you hadn't flung the cat among the pigeons." She pulled open the door into the entry and let it swing behind her, not caring—much—if it hit him in the face.

He followed. "Mine was an innocent enough question."

"Oh, please. Anyone with an awareness of modern Western civilization knows that schools and libraries and all sorts of institutions walk a fine line during the holidays. No matter what we do, someone will be unhappy."

"But this is little ol' Ridgeville, where there's a church on every other corner. I wouldn't expect you to have that kind of problem."

"As this morning demonstrated, however, we do. Now, if you'll excuse me—"

He caught her wrist as she turned away. "From what Sarah said, this 'bah, humbug' policy is new. I'm guessing it's a change you installed when you took over. What have you, per-sonally, got against Christmas?"

"Nothing. Nothing at all." If only she could maintain her poise as he stared at her.

"I don't believe you. Did you only get coal in your stock-ing as a kid?"

"We had very nice Christmases, thank you." She jerked her arm, trying to break free of his grip. "Let me go."

"Eventually." Instead, though, he backed up until he could sit on the third step of the marble staircase circling up to the second floor. And then he drew her close, and closer, until she could choose to stand between his knees or sit beside him. After last night, Jayne chose to sit, with several inches of marble between them.

"So tell me about what your family did for Christmas." Chris had turned toward her on the stair and was watching her face. "What kinds of special rituals did you follow?"

"I don't recall anything special. My family wasn't particu-larly…religious. We bought presents and a tree. That was it."

"What kind of decorations? Live tree or artificial?"

She'd come up against that blank wall in her mind again. "I really don't remember. It wasn't important."

"Oh, come on, Jayne. Everybody remembers Christmas, if they get it. Santa Claus and reindeer and cookies. Carols and colored lights. Dancing snowmen. What's your favorite?"

"I don't know!" She jerked hard, just as he let go of her wrist, and the momentum sent her staggering to her feet. With her cheeks burning and her eyes tearing she scurried to the office doorway, shut herself inside and locked the door.

Then she threw herself down on the sofa and buried her face in her arms.

Why, why, *why* couldn't she remember?

CHRIS PUT ON THE SAME clothes for the third day in a row and went down to the kitchen to check on the girls' cleanup job. Sarah must have gotten after them because the place looked crumb-free and neat enough even for Jayne Thomas.

Juliet Radcliffe had not been much for housekeeping.

The contrast didn't shake his conviction, however. Juliet had become Jayne, sometime after that disastrous Christmas Eve, the last time he saw her. And Jayne couldn't remember holidays with her make-believe family because she'd never had one. She should remember the penthouse apartment she'd told him about, the silver-trimmed artificial trees her parents rolled out of storage every year, the champagne-and-cocaine-fueled parties for Manhattan celebrities.

He could understand wanting to block those memories. But why not remember him, and Charlie and the grandmother she'd come to care about? Why create a complete fiction?

"Oh, hi." Beth hesitated in the kitchen doorway. "Where's Tommy?"

"Tommy? Is there another guy around here I don't know about? Can he lend me some clothes?"

She grinned. "Tommy is Ms. Thomas's nickname. We only call her that when she can't hear us."

"You think she doesn't know?"

The girl winked at him. "I think she wants us to think she doesn't know."

"I think you're right. Well, Tommy went to get dressed. And maybe take a breather from the responsibility for you young witches."

Again, she surprised him. "The only witch is Taryn, the pagan. I'm just Jewish."

"Right. What do you think about Christmas decorations?"

She shrugged. "I can cope. It's not like I've never heard the

Christmas story. And my uncle married a Christian." She whistled and shook her head. "Boy, were Nana and Poppi mad. But she's part of the family, and her kids celebrate Hanukkah and Christmas. Big deal."

"Then you should help with the negotiations. Maybe somehow you girls can come up with a compromise that makes everybody happy."

"Except Yolanda. She'll never give in."

"What's her problem?"

Wrong question. Beth literally backed up, into the hallway. "One of the rules here is that we don't talk about other girls. I gotta go find the crossword book I want before somebody else steals it." A second later she vanished into the library, leaving Chris with the proverbial egg on his face.

Not being a puzzle man himself, he didn't intend to spend the morning in the library, dutifully playing word games or piecing together edges. He'd already brought in enough firewood to handle a month-long blizzard. With the computers down and his cameras at Charlie's, his professional outlets had been blocked.

So he went for another walk in the snow, wearing boots that were still damp. Heading away from the manor and the tangled trails of yesterday's play, he forged a new path through the snow toward a cluster of cottages set at a distance from the main house. Yesterday, Jayne had told him they were originally used as quarters for a few superior servants, but the small houses now offered accommodation for guests and teachers at Hawkridge School.

The bright colors of the buildings—pink, blue, yellow and even lavender—made quite a contrast with the brilliant white of the snow, the dark green of the pines and spruces, garlanded with more snow, and the gray and black tracings of leafless tree branches. His fists clenched with the hunger for a camera. He wasn't used to taking pretty landscape shots, but the beauty of this setting begged to be preserved.

Years spent in the dirty snow of big cities and the sparsely forested Asian battlefields had left him empty, Chris realized. He'd forgotten how much he loved these mountains, in winter and summer. Forgotten, too, the pleasure of being with Charlie, who offered love and acceptance without making demands. And in forgetting, Chris had almost left it too late. The doctors had given Charlie less than a year to live.

As he trekked past the lavender cottage, Chris noticed a plaque on the post of the small front porch. Out of curiosity, he detoured to read the three lines on the sign: Jayne Thomas, Headmistress, The Hawkridge School.

"Well, well." From the sign, he took two strides across the porch to the front door, and was not surprised to find it unlocked. Security around this school was haphazard at best.

He left his boots in the snow and stepped inside wearing only his socks, despite the frigid temperature. Without central heat, the house was nearly as cold as the outdoors. The small entry hall offered entrance to a living room on the right and a dining room on the left, both sized to host a faculty party or a parent reception. Identical mantels graced the fireplace of each room, constructed with marble matching the stone of the staircase in the manor. The furniture complemented the age of the house, with late Victorian mahogany curves, seat covers in purple velvet, lots of thickly framed mirrors, and paintings of overblown flowers. Chris doubted this setting would have been Jayne's personal choice.

The doorway at the end of the entry hall led into a modernized kitchen left undecorated by its current user. Not even a dishcloth occupied the countertop. The den on the right offered leather chairs and wall-to-wall bookshelves with a TV cabinet in the center. The remaining walls were paneled and bare. Jayne had hung no photographs of any kind, as if she had no friends or family or pets. Surely she had pictures of her life at some point. Surely she'd traveled, studied, visited…something?

On the other side of the kitchen, a hallway led to a bathroom tiled in lavender, with plain white towels on the racks, but no lotions or perfumes on display. Ignoring his conscience, Chris opened the medicine cabinet to discover pain relievers, dental floss, toothpaste and toothbrush. Nothing personal. Nothing intimate.

Did Jayne Thomas exist at all?

Lavender walls shadowed the bedroom, but a white spread on the antique bed reflected light. A white blanket was folded neatly at the foot, with white pillowcases and sheets at the opposite end. Searching for color, Chris went through the chest of drawers, where navy blue proved a recurring theme for sweaters, turtlenecks and socks. In the closet, navy and black slacks and denim jeans hung beside navy dresses, black skirts and matching jackets, with matching shoes on the floor. The room was perfectly neat, perfectly clean. Practically empty.

Finally he sat down at the dressing table, an elegant piece with an oval mirror, a curved front and inlaid top and drawers. A silver brush, comb and hand mirror lay diagonally across the polished wood. EJT were the initials on the back of the mirror and the brush, in an old-fashioned script with the large *T* indicating the last name.

Chris blew out a long breath as if he'd run a race. He'd gleaned a single piece of information—the *E* would belong to her "grandmother." What else could he learn?

The center drawer contained handkerchiefs, starched and

ironed to a knife edge, embroidered with EJT. Under them lay a church bulletin. His hand shook as he picked it up.

"Village Methodist Church. Memorial Service for Elizabeth Jayne Thomas. July 14, 1992." Inside, the order of service listed hymns, Bible passages and a "Message of Hope." At the close of the service, Ms. Jayne Thomas invited the mourners to a reception at her grandmother's home on Mica Road.

"Hallelujah!" In his excitement, Chris barely avoided clutching the paper in his fist. Now he had a town, names and an address. He could—

Halfway out of the chair, he remembered he couldn't really do much of anything, trapped as he was by three feet of snow on the road. Sliding the bulletin back where he found it, he looked through the other drawers, where Jayne kept her lotions, a perfume called Tryst, of which he very much approved, and her plain cotton underwear, bras and panties.

He remembered Juliet's preference for wild prints and scanty styles. But he didn't doubt anymore.

The information he'd gained would be useful as he tried to pry Jayne from the colorless, featureless present she currently occupied. Someone—maybe Elizabeth Jayne, the so-called grandmother—had tried to create a past. Had she died before she could help Jayne develop a present?

And who would be helping Jayne shape her future?

Chapter Seven

Despite his injured shoulder, Chris had taken a snow shovel to the front staircase of the Manor. While the girls stayed inside, he'd cleared the individual treads and a wide section of the terrace at the top.

Now Jayne sat on one of the bare steps, watching the girls play in the late-afternoon sunlight.

"They're like bees out there, buzzing from one place to the other." Chris dropped down beside her. "What do you suppose they're talking about?"

"If I had to bet, I'd say Christmas." She gave him a sidelong glance that expressed more than a trace of the morning's irritation. "Thanks to you."

"That's not a bad thing, is it?"

"At least they aren't fighting…. Wait, I spoke too soon." An argument had broken out between Yolanda and Taryn. The snow figure Taryn had been working on for the last hour lost its head. Then Yolanda got a fistful of snow in the face.

Jayne started to stand, but Chris grabbed her arm. "Let them settle it."

"They're more likely to embroil the rest of the girls in a full-scale war." She stood up too quickly and her feet immediately slid out from beneath her, so she sat down hard again, with the edge of a step in her back.

Or there would have been if Chris hadn't put his arm between her and the sharp stone.

She pivoted toward him even as she heard his hiss of pain. "Are you okay?" Leaning forward, she helped him ease his arm out from behind her. "Did I break the bone?"

He grinned. "You aren't that heavy. Anyway, this coat's pretty thick. I'm more worried about you."

"I'm fine." And she was—more than fine, in fact, as she sat with her knees pressed into Chris's side, her hand on his thigh and his shoulder firm against her chest. His face was only a few inches away, close enough to show her the flecks of icy-white and coal-black in those bright blue eyes, the heavy texture of his thick lashes, the surprising smoothness of his skin beneath the stubble. "You're going to have a regular beard before the snow clears," she murmured.

"How do you feel about that?" His voice rumbled along her nerves, to fingertips and toes and deep into her belly.

Why did he care why she cared? "I—"

"Ms. Thomas!" The shout jerked her awake like a splash of frigid water.

"Coming!" She surged to her feet with no clumsiness at all and started toward the huddle of girls in the snow.

Striding along the cleared path to the lawn, then sidestepping down the slope, Jayne indulged in a silent rant. Either Yolanda or Taryn had probably drawn blood by now, because they weren't being properly supervised by the one person they'd been taught to depend on.

How could she have made so many stupid mistakes all at once? Forgetting her dignity, ignoring her responsibilities, abandoning her principles—she must be losing her mind. Because of Chris Hammond.

Taking a deep breath, she broke through the huddle of students. "Okay, let's just calm down…"

But Yolanda and Taryn were still on their feet, side by side. In the center of the ring of girls was Sarah, kneeling beside Haley, who sat on the ground with her arm cradled against her.

Jayne knelt on her other side. "What happened?"

Haley raised a tearstained face. "I slipped and fell backward. Now my arm hurts."

Holding back a sigh at the child's overreaction, Jayne put a hand on Haley's knee. "Does anything else hurt? Your legs? Your back? Your head?" Haley shook her head three times, and Jayne smiled. "Good. We'll help you up, and then I'll walk you inside—"

Haley shook her head again. "I can't walk."

Alarm fluttered in Jayne's chest. "You said your legs don't hurt."

"But when I move, my arm hurts really, really bad. Maybe Mr. Hammond could carry me?"

Jayne choked back a chuckle. "Mr. Hammond has his own hurt shoulder, remember? And he's already overextended himself shoveling the steps. I think Sarah and I can help you walk without too much pain for your arm. Let's give it a try."

Haley took the suggestion badly and sobbed most of the way to the stairs, then shrieked with each minor jolt as they ascended to the terrace. Chris held the door open and shut it when the last girl got inside.

Haley stopped them all in the center of the entry hall. Staring up at the second floor, she whined, "Do I have to climb all those steps?"

Jayne fought back a roll of her eyes. "Let's look at your arm first. Maybe you don't need the infirmary."

Sarah herded the other girls underneath the staircase and toward the storeroom to take off their coats. Jayne led Haley into the office. "I'll help you slip out of your coat and gloves and then see what we've got."

What they had, she saw at once, was more complicated than she'd hoped. Haley's wrist was swollen and red.

"You've definitely got a bruise," she said, touching the skin gently with one finger. "Possibly a sprain." She glanced at Chris over her shoulder. "What do you think?"

He crouched in front of Haley. His blunt fingers, handling the childish wrist, seemed gentle and sure. "I'd say definitely a sprain." Looking up into Haley's tear-streaked face, he smiled. "I think ice is what we need. Fortunately, we've got mountains full of the stuff."

The resulting giggle surprised Jayne. She would never have gotten such a reaction. But then, Chris Hammond's smile was a powerful force, as she knew all too well.

"A great idea," she said. "I'll walk you down to the kitchen."

Haley sniffed again. "Could you help me, Mr. Hammond?"

He straightened up and took a step back. "*I'm* going to fetch a bucket of snow. I suspect Tommy…er, Ms. Thomas will take good care of you. She knows where everything is." Avoiding her glare at his use of the forbidden nickname, he sidled out the office door.

Half an hour later, Haley had been settled into one of the soft leather chairs nearest the fireplace, with her feet on an equally soft ottoman and the injured arm wrapped in a towel within plastic bags of snow. A mug of hot chocolate and a plate of cookies sat within reach of her good hand. Taryn lounged on the floor on one side of the ottoman, Selena on the other. The rest of the girls were cozily arranged near the hearth, enjoying the fire's warmth and the sweet snack as blue shadows crept across the snow beyond the window at Jayne's shoulder.

Haley set her mug down and looked across at Chris, who was straddling his usual chair. "Tell us more of the story, Mr. Hammond."

Jayne cleared her throat. "I believe that should be a request, not a royal order. And perhaps now isn't the best time."

"Please, would you tell us more, Mr. Hammond?" Haley's voice could scarcely be heard above the pleas of the others joining in.

And Chris, damn him, was happy to oblige. "I'll make this installment short, since dinnertime isn't too far away."

"I'll start cooking," Jayne said, heading for the library door. An adolescent romance was the last thing she wanted to think about. In fact, she would prefer to avoid thoughts of romance altogether.

But the girls protested her departure. "You can sit here," Sarah said, scooting toward the middle of the couch and patting the end cushion. "There's plenty of room. And this is a warm spot."

Jayne couldn't refuse the sweet invitation. "Just don't blame me when you get hungry." She made a show of getting comfortable, then looked at the man across the carpet. "Whenever you're ready."

The gleam in his eye told her he knew she didn't want to stay. And why. "Very good. I think we'd reached the point where Juliet had come back to the mountains for the summer."

"And she and Chase were going to have all kinds of adventures," Haley interjected.

"Exactly. Juliet managed to get away from her grandmother's house almost every day without letting anyone know where she would be spending time. And since he couldn't think of anything else to do, Chase included her in his explorations."

Three summers and winters passed as Chase and Juliet grew from kids into teenagers. During the Christmas holidays they played in the snow, skiing and sledding and building forts for snowball fights. Summers were long but not lazy. They paddled Charlie's canoe in nearby creeks and streams, and hiked as many of the park trails as they could reach on bicycles.

On hot days, they swam in the pond behind Charlie's house or in the reservoir that gave Ridgeville its water. All kinds of berries came into season and they picked their share, along with apples, peaches and pears. Charlie paid them to weed his garden, and the money bought them tickets to the only movie theater in town. After they ate dinner with Charlie, Chase would bike home with Juliet. The first time, she introduced him to the German shepherds, Helga and Gretchen, who turned out to be big babies when they knew you.

Most nights, after Juliet went into the house for dinner with her grandmother, she came back to the woods inside the big iron gate, where Chase waited with the dogs. They spent the evening hours climbing trees or watching the stars wheel across the mountain sky. Sometimes they talked, but they were good enough friends that they didn't have to say a word.

On the first night of August in the year they both turned fifteen, they were lying on their backs in the grass, watching stars pop into the sky.

"I have to go home next week," Juliet said, and sighed. "School starts the sixteenth."

"That sucks." Chase couldn't think of the words to express how much he would hate seeing her leave. So he said as little as possible.

She threw a stone into the air and caught it again. "I think we should do something really fantastic first."

"Like what?"

"Bungee jumping."

He snorted. "Who wants to take a dive and not hit the water? That's dumb."

"Okay. Parachuting?"

"Costs a hundred dollars, at least. I don't have it, if you do. Anyway, you have to be eighteen or twenty-one or something."

"Oh." After a minute, she turned on her side to face him. "Then I think we should spend a night outdoors."

This time he shrugged. "That's no big deal. I sleep on Charlie's porch all the time."

"Not in town, stupid. I think we should climb up into the mountains and spend the night there."

He rolled over to look at her. "You're crazy."

That comment only made her more determined. By the end of the argument, Chase had agreed only because Juliet threatened to go without him. He knew Charlie would kill him if he let her go alone.

Of course, he also knew he should tell Charlie about the plan and let his granddad put a stop to it. But Chase wasn't a chicken or a snitch. Anyway, he could handle himself in the woods. They'd be safe enough, and he'd have a great adventure to take back to school with him in the fall.

With plenty of provisions in their backpacks and a casual goodbye to his granddad, they set off that morning as if it was any other day. Leaving their bikes locked to the rack at the ranger's station, they took the trail headed for the summit of Little Bear, where they'd decided to spend the night. The day was standard for the Blue Ridge Mountains in summer—a cool mist hung over them all morning as they hiked the steep path. When they stopped for lunch at a scenic overlook, they couldn't see ten feet past the edge of the wall.

"I hope it clears soon." Juliet finished her sandwich and tossed the wrapper into the trash can. "Two points for me. If we get nothing but fog we might as well have stayed in the valley."

"It'll clear," Chase said, with more confidence than he felt. He threw his potato-chip bag at the can…and missed.

"I win." Juliet grinned, picked up his bag and threw it away. "Let's get moving."

Shaking his head, Chase followed her. He wondered if he would ever be cool. Would Juliet still like him if he never was?

The clouds began to lift about an hour later. Soon the sun shone warm and bright, giving them great views of the blue mountains and the green valleys below. Juliet took off the sweater she'd worn in the chilly morning, revealing a short black tank top that hugged her curves and showed more bare female skin than Chase had ever seen, even in her bathing suit. He took off his sweatshirt, too, but he couldn't be sure whether it was the sun or Juliet that had warmed him up.

At three-thirty, they reached a level spot with a stone bench set against the mountain, and a walled overlook revealing a straight drop down for a thousand feet.

"Listen to this." Juliet stood in front of the sign posted above the trail marker. "'The remainder of the Little Bear Trail requires climbing as well as hiking, going up and coming down. Do not attempt to reach the summit unless you are comfortable with vertical heights and can use your arms to support your weight.'" She turned to Chase. "Sounds awesome."

"Sounds hard. Are you sure you want to do this?"

"You think you can climb better than me?"

"Yeah." He didn't back down this time.

Juliet laughed and nodded. "Okay, you probably can. But I'll be okay. Let's go."

Before he could stop her, she strode up the path and around a bend, leaving him no option but to follow.

"That sign wasn't kidding," she panted, a bit farther on. They were finding roots and rocks with their hands to help pull them up the trail. "Too bad we've already been hiking all day."

He knew she was getting tired. And he'd noticed storm clouds gathering on top of the higher mountains. "Let's turn around, Juli. We don't want to spend the night in the rain."

"I thought we would find a cave." She ignored the suggestion to stop.

After a flatter section gave them a chance to catch their breath, they came to the next climb, which looked absolutely vertical.

Staring up, Chase shook his head. "Not worth it at this point in the day. And there's not enough shelter here to stay the night. We're going back." He started walking down the way they'd just come.

"You can be a wuss if you want to. I'm not."

He jerked around and saw Juliet already ten feet up the climb. "Damn it, Juli. Why can't you just give in?"

She didn't answer, but kept climbing. As Chase stood at the bottom, gathering his own energy to make the effort, a softball-size rock came hurtling at his head.

"Hey," he cried, looking up. "Watch out—"
Juliet screamed. Then she fell.

The girls in the library were sitting forward, literally on the edge of their seats. When Chris didn't say anything else, their eyes widened.

"Is that it?" Beth demanded. "Is that where he killed her?"

"You can't quit now," Monique told him. "Just keep talking."

Chris shrugged. "I said I'd keep it short."

"Well, that's too short," Yolanda stated. "Don't leave us hanging in midair."

He glanced at Jayne, who seemed as mesmerized as the rest.

"Well, okay...."

Chase managed to be under Juliet when she fell, but he wouldn't have said he caught her. They both went down hard on the rocky ground, with him on the bottom.

"Oh, God, Chase, are you okay?" She got to her knees beside him, put her hands on his shoulder and shook him. "Please say you're not dead."

He groaned and opened his eyes. "I would be, if I had a broken spine and you shook me like that. Let go." Lying still for a few seconds, he located the source of the pain throbbing through him. "My shoulder. It's killing me."

"Is it broken?"

"Maybe. I don't know." He tried to move his arm and almost passed out. "I can't climb anymore. We've got to go back."

"Rest for a little while first. Have some water." Juliet slipped off her backpack, then froze. "I forgot. The water's in your pack."

He rolled his eyes. "Great. Just great. You'll have to take it off. No—don't drag the straps over my shoulders. Unclip them instead." Even that simple process made his shoulder scream, but he survived. They each drank a bottle of water and ate a candy bar. Then, with Chase dragging his backpack, they started down the trail.

At the steep portion, he swallowed hard. "This…is gonna be tough."

Juliet wiped tears off her cheeks. "I'm so sorry. I didn't mean to get you hurt. What can I do? How can I help?"

He couldn't stand it when she cried, because it didn't happen often. "Well, I could climb on your back," he suggested, "and you could carry me down to the station."

That made her laugh. "And then I'd make up a story about how I wanted to turn back, but you kept on climbing and then fell and hurt your shoulder, so I'd be the hero who got you to safety again."

"You probably would."

"I definitely would." She looked down the path again. "Are you gonna make it?"

Before he could answer, the clouds opened up. Buckets of rain dumped onto their side of the mountain, right on their heads. The wind lashed around them and thunder rolled, as if it was the end of the world.

Soaked to the skin, his teeth chattering and his arm numb, Chase couldn't think for a minute. Then he remembered. "In my bag. A plastic sheet. We can sit under it."

Juliet found the sheet and they held it over their heads as they sat with their backs against a small pine tree.

"How long do you think it will last?" she asked. There were goose bumps on every inch of her bare skin.

"No telling." He was watching water rush down the trail as if it were Niagara Falls. They were stuck till the storm passed. Even then, he wasn't sure he could make the climb one-handed.

After a while, Juliet remembered her sweater and tugged it on. She pulled out Chase's sweatshirt and laid it across his chest, with the arms around his neck and hanging down in back.

Then she scooted in close to his uninjured side. "I'll put my arm like this," she said, sliding it behind his waist. "Think you'll be warm enough?"

That one move took care of the problem. "I'm fine."

Chase thought he'd gotten used to her in shorts this summer, but the tank top added to the shorts packed a mighty punch. He propped his right foot against the ground, keeping his knee bent, just in case he couldn't get his attention on something besides the press of Juliet's chest against him.

Meanwhile, the longest thunderstorm in Blue Ridge Mountain history raged on.

After a few minutes, Juliet stirred. "My legs are cold. Would you mind if I tucked my knees under yours?"

This time, Chase didn't hide his groan. "Are you trying to kill me?"

She stared at him. "What?"

He blew out a breath. "Juliet…" The words wouldn't come. "Never mind."

She scooted her knees under his raised one, tucking her thighs up against his butt. And then, of course, she put her head on his shoulder.

"That's nice," she purred.

Behind his closed lids, Chase rolled his eyes. *Nice. Right.*

They sat for a long time, waiting for the rain to stop. Chase fell asleep with his head against the tree trunk. When he opened his eyes again, the rain had slowed from a deluge to a shower.

But the sun had set behind the mountains. There was no way they were leaving this place tonight.

Taking a deep breath, he decided he didn't care. They'd be warm enough under the sheet, especially together like this. He moved his head a little and realized he'd shifted slightly, resting his cheek on top of Juliet's head. He chuckled.

She turned her face to his. "What are you laughing at?"

"I was thinking it's a good thing the rain washed those spikes out of your hair. My cheek would have had holes in it."

She smiled, her pouty mouth like a curve of raspberry sauce in her pale face. Chase loved raspberries. So he bent his head far enough to kiss her.

The world could have ended there and he wouldn't have cared. Kissing Juliet was the best thing that had ever happened in his life, or ever would happen. The big hole inside of him, the crater carved by years of listening to his parents curse each other and him, healed over in that moment. He was whole again, and free. Anything he wanted to do was possible.

All because Juliet kissed him.

Chris stopped there. He didn't trust himself to say anything else. He'd never shared this memory, not even with Juliet. She'd always been a little skittish, he realized, to hear how he felt about that first kiss. He'd never been quite sure of her, even when he held her in his arms.

For a long time, the only sound in the library was the crackle and pop of the logs in the fireplace. As much as he wanted to look at Jayne, he didn't dare. He could only hope the force of his feelings was somehow shaking the foundation of hers.

Not surprisingly, she was the first person to move. Without a sound, she rose from her corner of the couch and left the library. Chris expected to hear the noise of banging pans and clattering dishes. But the silence stretched for another moment.

Then the girls began moving, whispering, sharing their responses to the story with each other. They didn't approach Chris and he didn't intrude. Right now, they all needed the distance. As did he.

He didn't look for Jayne, either, even when he realized she wasn't in the kitchen. She'd gone somewhere to hide. Her office, maybe, or the women's bathroom.

Good. That meant he'd stirred something inside of her—memories, hopefully. Emotions. Passions.

God knew, she'd already done the same for him.

JAYNE PROPPED HER HANDS on the sink in the bathroom attached to her office and let her head hang from her shoulders. Without heat, the tiled space felt like a refrigerator. The cold water she'd splashed on her face and hands and wrists would start to crystallize any moment now.

She welcomed the icy burn on her red, overheated face. What was wrong with her? How could she get so wrapped up in the story that she'd forgotten where she was, even who she was? Sitting in the midst of her students, the children she should be taking care of, she'd lost all sense of herself to become a crazy, undisciplined teenager.

That, she knew, had never happened. She'd been a good girl, her grandmother had told her, a straight-A student who babysat in the afternoons and taught Sunday school to fourth graders. Never, ever had she run wild with some boy in the mountains, staying out all night, letting him kiss her. Jayne Thomas wouldn't do that.

But Jayne Thomas had let Chris Hammond kiss her. He'd put his hands on her skin. She had touched him, too. And that was the real problem. Somehow she'd confused those moments the other night with the story he'd told today, and her reactions had gotten tangled, twined together. He'd probably done it deliberately, thinking he could seduce her again, using his words as a kind of verbal foreplay.

What made her angry was that it had worked. At that moment, he could have taken anything she had to give.

But not anymore. Jayne straightened her back, grabbed a brush out of the vanity drawer and dragged it through her hair, then twisted the ponytail holder ruthlessly tight. Leaving the last chill droplets on her face, she picked up her flashlight and made her way back to the hallway. There she took a deep breath and squared her shoulders.

After dinner, she'd get the girls into their bedrolls early. With any luck, they wouldn't need another episode of the Chase and Juliet soap opera tonight. If worse came to worst, Jayne would sit in the farthest corner and read a book on her own. She didn't have to listen to Chris Hammond. She didn't have to kiss him.

And she certainly didn't have to fall in love with him.

Chapter Eight

Chris kept Haley company while Jayne supervised the rest of the girls in constructing a chicken-and-rice dinner cooked on the fire.

Conversation lagged until they'd all eased the worst of their hunger pangs. Even then, the mood at the table stayed somber, in part because Jayne made none of her usual efforts to stimulate a discussion. She sat quiet and withdrawn as he and the girls finished up their first helpings and passed the serving bowl around for seconds.

Selena emptied her glass of milk, set it down with a thud, then looked at her headmistress. "Ms. Thomas, about Christmas…"

Jayne jumped, but rallied quickly. "I think we've covered that already, Selena."

"Well, but we've been talking about it today. And we have a plan."

"A plan?"

"Most of us want some kind of decorations," Beth said, leaning forward to speak around Yolanda.

"Not me." Yolanda waved a hand, dismissing the idea. "I'm not having any part of this." But then she let her arm drop. "I won't get in the way. And I won't stay in my room," she said, when Jayne started to speak. "I can deal."

The headmistress did not look reassured. "Still, I think—"

"You haven't heard the plan." Monique received a stern look from Jayne for the interruption, and ducked her head. "I'm sorry. But we'd really like to have a celebration, do some decorating, maybe have some cookies and a special dinner. But we don't intend to impose any one way of believing on anybody."

Jayne propped her chin in her hand. "What is it you want to do?"

The details poured out. During the cleanup, while Yolanda washed dishes so the sound of running water would drown out the voices, the girls explained their plans and added embellishments.

"You'll help, won't you, Mr. Hammond?" Haley had been exempted from cleanup and was sitting beside Chris as he finished his coffee. "We need someone to do the sawing."

"That's up to Ms. Thomas." He tipped the rim of his mug toward Jayne, who remained at the other end of the table, contrary to her habit of helping the girls straighten up. "She has the final say."

"I think…" She squeezed her eyes closed for a moment, then opened them and gripped her own mug more tightly. "Since you all are so excited and pleased with your ideas, and since Yolanda feels she can deal with whatever you're planning, I don't think it would be fair of me to stand in the way. Certainly, we can have a holiday celebration."

"With decorations?" Selena clasped the dish she was drying against her chest. "And everything?"

"As long as nothing in the house is damaged. And you'll need to be careful about where you do your sawing." Finally, a small smile curved her lips. "The groundskeeper won't be happy if you cut down one of his prize evergreens."

"We won't!" The happy chatter continued as the students went to their rooms to change for bed.

Chris took a sip of coffee as he studied Jayne at the other end of the table. "They seem to have reached a reasonable compromise on their own."

"Yes, I guess they have."

"You're not happy about it?"

"I'm quite pleased that they could work together and make a decision that benefits nearly everyone."

"Except Yolanda."

"Yes."

"And you."

She looked up from her coffee mug. "That's...I don't know what you mean."

"You don't want a celebration of any kind."

She shrugged. "I'll survive."

"What do you have against Christmas?"

"Nothing."

"Did your grandmother beat you on Christmas Day?"

"Of course not."

"Did she go to church?"

"Y-yes, we attended services for Christmas."

"Have you been since she died?"

Her gaze sharpened. "How did you know she was dead?"

Big mistake. "You mentioned it."

"I didn't."

"How else would I get that information? I can't do any Internet research. I can't get to town to ask questions."

Judging by her frown, Jayne obviously didn't want to let go of her suspicions. "I simply don't enjoy the holiday, okay? I don't have family left to celebrate with and I'm usually at school with students. The religious significance of Christmas has been buried under commercialism and diluted by political correctness. Could you please just accept my reasons and move on?"

She stood abruptly and went to the sink. Chris didn't respond until she'd washed, dried and put away her mug. Then he got to his feet.

"I don't think I can do that." He walked toward her. "There are too many unanswered questions about you, Jayne Thomas. I need to know the truth."

"You can't handle the truth," she growled, imitating a well-known movie line delivered by a famous actor. But her grin faded quickly. "You won't *accept* the truth, Chris. You think there's some big mystery about me, but there's not. I'm just plain Jayne Thomas."

She had tilted her chin to look up at him. Chris set his fingertips on the column of her throat. "Jayne, maybe. Plain…not a chance." As he slid his hand around to cup the nape of her neck, he lowered his head to take her mouth with a kiss.

Jayne whimpered and pushed against his shoulder. "The girls," she whispered.

"We'll hear them." He hoped so, at least. But the way the feel of her took over him, he could stay lost in her lips, in her scent and taste and touch, for hours. Forever.

He put his arm around her and she yielded, pressing her body against his, spreading her warm hands over his chest. Her lush mouth was a wonder in itself, more experienced than last night, more experimental, as if she'd been thinking about kissing and the variations she wanted to try. Chris was happy to provide her with the opportunity to practice.

One minute, he and Jayne stood as if melded together, tongues mating, hands against flesh, breaths heated and fast. In the next instant, she was leaning into the refrigerator, intent on rearranging…whatever. Chris planted himself at the window with his back to the room, plunging his fists into his pockets for good measure as the gaggle of girls returned.

"The sky is clouding up." He had to clear his throat twice to make his voice work. "We might get more snow tonight."

Haley came to stand beside him, peering into the darkness. "It will have to stop by morning. We need to get a Yule log."

"So you've decided to call this celebration Yule?"

"YuleChristakkah," Sarah said, joining them.

"Or maybe HanYuleMas," Beth added, grinning.

"ChrisHanYule?" Selena suggested.

Monique put her hands on her hips. "Want to add some Kwanzaa to that word?" But she wasn't really mad.

Their good spirits persisted even when Jayne suggested an early bedtime in the library. Chris listened with a smile as the girls gently teased each other.

Only Jayne seemed removed from the communion. She sat in the farthest corner from the fire, pretending to read the book in her lap. Chris, keeping watch, didn't see her turn a single page.

What was she thinking? Did that frown on her face, the line between her brows, pertain to the present or the past?

As the chatter died away, Haley turned to face the fireplace. "Can we get some more of the story now? Did Chase and Juliet get rescued? Or did they die together on the mountain?"

Chris looked over at Jayne, who gave him a nod. "They didn't die. When Chase didn't show up for dinner, Charlie was concerned, of course, as was Juliet's grandmother. And since she was actually a very smart lady, she had already figured out where Juliet spent her days, and who to call when Juliet didn't come home.

"By the next morning, the whole town was up in the state

park, looking for the lost teenagers. Not more than two hours passed before the rescue squad found them."

"And they both got yelled at." Selena settled into her pillows. "I would have been grounded forever."

"Yes, they got yelled at. And grounded. But they saw each other again before school started. And when Christmas came, when the next summer arrived, Chase and Juliet didn't worry so much about seeking adventure in the mountains.

"They'd discovered, you see, that the real source of all the excitement, all the magic in the world, was the time they spent together. Alone."

In summing up this chapter of his story, Chris allowed his voice to drone. One by one the girls dropped off to sleep, until only he and Jayne were left awake in the room.

Even she, he realized when he stopped, had surrendered. Her head rested against the broad wing of the armchair and she snored softly, her mouth open.

Watching her, Chris chuckled. He'd have to remember to warn her, when they slept together, that he snored, too.

JAYNE JERKED AWAKE, gasping for breath. Across the dark library the giant fireplace glowed with orange light. The heat fell far short of where she sat, however, and her fingers and feet were stiff with cold. Even her face felt frozen. When she touched her cheeks, she gathered tears. Her chin dripped with them.

She hadn't yet taken to carrying her grandmother's handkerchiefs in her pockets, so she pulled up the hem of her knit shirt to wipe her face and nose. What in the world had she been dreaming? Why would she wake up crying and afraid?

As hard as she tried, she couldn't recall the dream, or the least suspicion of what had scared her. The blank wall was there, as impenetrable as ever.

She got out of the chair, wincing as her cold feet took her weight. Hobbling to the door, she stopped to count the bodies on the floor and realized one girl was absent. Her heart jumped into her throat, but she choked back the urge to worry. None of them could get into much trouble with three feet of snow outside.

"Make that four," she commented to herself as she stood once again at the kitchen window. Chris's prediction of more snow had been quite accurate. Huge flakes were falling through the black night. Tomorrow, all the footprints they'd made would be filled with fresh powder.

"Wonderful." Jayne sipped from the mug of juice she'd poured for herself. "Just wonderful."

"Ms. Thomas?" She jumped as a voice spoke from the kitchen doorway. "Sorry—I didn't mean to scare you." Neither of them had bothered to carry a flashlight, but Jayne could always distinguish Yolanda's smoky voice and Louisiana accent.

"That's okay. I forgot someone else was up." Jayne went to the counter for a napkin to blot juice from her sweater. "Trouble sleeping?"

"A little. Can I have some milk?"

"Sure." Jayne poured a glass and they sat down across the table from one another. "What's bothering you?"

"Besides more snow?"

"You don't like snow?"

Yolanda shrugged. "I liked it the first day. Now it's starting to wear on my nerves."

"I understand. I don't like snow at all."

"And now…well, never mind."

Jayne risked a guess. "The decorations?"

"Yeah." She cleared her throat. "I mean, yes, ma'am. I don't look forward to having the place all jazzed up."

"I understood there wouldn't be any Nativity scenes."

"I know. But that's the whole reason for Christmas, right? This baby was born and everybody's supposed to be joyful…"

Jayne couldn't see clearly in the darkness, but she could hear the tears in Yolanda's voice. "Does Christmas make you think of your babies?"

A sob was the only answer. Jayne walked around the table and sat next to the teen, putting her arm around the shaking body and gently pressing the wet face against her shoulder.

"I'm sorry," Yolanda gasped, between crying jags.

"You have nothing to be sorry for."

"I killed my babies. How could I do that?"

"You were eleven the first time and thirteen the second. That's too young to be a mother." Jayne lightly stroked Yolanda's soft, short curls. "You couldn't give either of them the home and family a baby needs."

"I could've let somebody else adopt them."

She didn't argue with that conclusion. "You can't suffer over this forever. You have to forgive yourself."

"Would they forgive me? My two babies?"

This time, the answer came easily. "Yes, I believe they would." She shifted to gaze into Yolanda's face. "What you have to do now is live the rest of your life in a way that shows how much you care. We all make mistakes. Our responsibility is to become better, wiser people because of those mistakes. It's when we don't learn and improve that our flaws and errors can be held against us."

"It's so hard."

Jayne nodded. "But you're strong. You can do anything you set your mind and heart on."

They sat silent in the dark until Yolanda yawned. "Maybe I can get some sleep now. It's warmer in there, anyway. I'm freezing to death."

"Me, too." They put their mug and glass in the sink and walked together to the library.

The girl turned at the door. "You're terrific," she whispered, leaning over to kiss Jayne's cheek. "Hawkridge and you are the best things that ever happened to me."

Smiling, Jayne returned the hug. "Go get warm. I'm going to curl up on the couch with my blanket."

Despite the warmth of the fire and the heavy blanket, oblivion didn't come as easily as she'd hoped. Her mind seemed to be full of echoes, fragments of voices and noises she didn't know or understand. When at last she did fall asleep, the echoes followed, chasing her through forests and across snow-covered fields, driving her into freezing cold rivers and down briar-covered hills until at last she ran straight into that familiar blank wall.

The shock jolted her awake. She sat up, eyes wide, heart pounding. Twice more she settled herself into a doze, but the shards of dreams continued to trouble her. Each time, the collision with that wall brought about an abrupt, fearful awakening. Finally, Jayne lay motionless and sleepless on the couch, staring at the dwindling fire and waiting for dawn to arrive.

As a result, she wasn't in a good mood when the girls awoke a couple of hours later. Irritated by their busy chatter about the decorations they had planned, she said almost nothing during yet another breakfast of cereal and milk.

"You okay, Ms. Thomas?" Monique sat down next to her. "You're looking a little pale."

"I'm fine." She used her willpower to produce a cheerful smile. "I'm just thinking about the first breakfast I'll make when the electricity comes on again—fried eggs, bacon, grits and biscuits. All piping hot."

"Sounds good. I'm pretty tired of oatmeal, myself." Monique let a spoonful of porridge plop back into her bowl. "Speaking of food, I'm in charge of our holiday dinner. What can we cook that's special? Do we have a turkey? A big, juicy roast? How will we make mashed potatoes without a mixer?"

They finally decided that roast chicken was their best option. Potatoes could be baked on the coals, and Jayne thought she could create a dessert with fruit, instant pudding and whipping cream. After cleaning up the kitchen, the girls went to dress for more outside play. Too weary even to get herself another cup of coffee, Jayne folded her arms on the table and put her head down. If she could just sleep for an hour…

"Is this the indefatigable Tommy Thomas I see before me?" Chris stood at the entrance to the kitchen, leaning one shoulder against the doorjamb. "Every time I look lately, you're falling asleep."

"That's because you aren't around in the middle of the night, when I can't sleep at all." Jayne ran her hands over her hair, hoping it didn't look too mussed. She hadn't yet done any real grooming this morning. "Come to think of it, I haven't had a decent night's rest since you arrived. I'm beginning to think it's all your fault." She got up from the table to refill her coffee. "And don't call me that."

"The girls do, when you're not around."

"That's their privilege as students."

"Then I'll just call you a grouch." He advanced to the coffeepot and poured himself a mug. "Looks like the girls are ready to hit the snow."

"Oh, yes." She didn't have to pretend a shiver. "Another wonderful morning spent standing in the cold."

He put a hand on her shoulder. "Listen, I think you could use some time to yourself. Why don't you stay inside for a couple of hours while I watch the girls? I promise I won't let anything happen to any of them."

Tears stung her eyes, and she took a quick sip of coffee to hide them. "That's a very nice suggestion."

"But?"

"But they are my responsibility. If anything happened and I wasn't there, the explanations, the repercussions..." She shook her head. "I don't know how I'm going to explain your presence here, as it is."

"You were the Good Samaritan who sheltered me after I crashed at your gate. We can't be blamed that a big blizzard showed up at the same time."

"And you have been very helpful," she conceded. "I doubt we'd have kept the fire going so well without you."

"Gee, I'm so glad to hear that."

His sarcastic tone turned her to face him. "Why are you upset?"

He gave a sullen, one-shouldered shrug. "I don't see myself as the Boy Scout type."

"You'd rather bully me into admitting I'm someone else?"

"You *are* Juliet."

"I thought you'd given up on this craziness."

"I'm waiting for you to recognize the truth."

They glared at each other while excited voices approached down the hallway.

Jayne snapped free of his gaze at the last possible moment and focused on the students, instead. "You all look ready for a morning of snow angels and sledding."

Selena took a step forward. "Actually, what we'd really like is to go ahead and start getting stuff from the woods for our decorations. You know—holly and pinecones and branches. Plus, we're having a Yule tree." She glanced at Taryn and Beth, on either side of her, for support. "We need to find a good one and we were hoping Mr. Hammond would cut it down for us."

Chris nodded. "I'll be glad to help. Let me get my coat and gloves."

He left the kitchen even as Jayne registered the fact that he hadn't checked with her for permission before agreeing.

"I'll get dressed and meet you by the door," she told the girls. Chris Hammond might think he could handle seven "little" girls by himself, but all he had to work with was a sexy smile and some well-built muscles.

She—Jayne Thomas, holder of a Ph.D. in counseling and social work, with a speciality in adolescent education, licensed in the state as a certified social worker and certified family therapist—was the ultimate authority in this school, the source of discipline and decisions. That was her role in life, her identity, however much Chris Hammond might wish she was someone else.

And however much she might wish he could see her—want her, even love her—as herself.

Chapter Nine

Once outside, the girls decided to start the hunt for their "Yule tree" immediately. Chris walked at the front of the group with the ax he'd found in the tool room over his good shoulder. Jayne brought up the rear of the procession, keeping her distance despite the fact that he didn't know where he should look for a tree on the vast Hawkridge estate.

Selena trudged beside him. "Ms. Thomas says we should follow the long trail toward Hawk's Ridge overlook. There will be trees we can choose from there."

"Sounds good, but for the part where I don't know the Hawk's Ridge trail. I haven't spent much time here at the school."

"The trail starts at the edge of the forest behind the dormitory." They plowed through the unmarked snow without talking for a few minutes, working hard as the ground sloped upward in front of them. On a short stretch of even ground, Selena said, "Do you live in Ridgeville, then?"

"Just visiting."

"For the first time?"

"Uh, no. I've been here before."

The girl smiled. "I thought so."

He'd given himself away, Chris knew. By tonight, all the

girls would understand that the story he was telling them was his own. But would they identify Juliet as Jayne?

"My mother will never believe I'm walking through the woods in the snow, looking for a Christmas tree to cut down." Selena glanced over her shoulder toward Beth and Taryn. "I mean, Yule tree."

"Right. Where are you from?"

"Los Angeles."

"Yeah, I guess they don't get too many white Yules."

"Nope. It's usually sunny and eighty degrees in December."

"This will be something to remember when you go back."

She didn't say anything for a moment. "I can't go back to L.A., or even California."

"Why not?"

There was another long pause as they waited for the rest of the crowd to catch up with them at the head of the trail. Selena focused on brushing snow from a nearby pine branch. "I was involved with…a gang. My boyfriend…he said the only way I could leave him would be to die."

"That's a tough choice."

"I didn't make it." She glanced at him, and her dark eyes flashed. "My mother had me abducted and brought here. I tried to run away three times that first month."

"How long have you been here?"

"Three years. Since seventh grade."

"You changed your mind about the gang."

She nodded. "Tommy helped me. Along with the other teachers and the counselors and the friends I made. Hawk-ridge is a good place."

"Looks like." The other girls filtered past them and Selena joined the hunt for the perfect tree. Chris didn't wait for Jayne to catch up with him, but walked on slowly by himself, enjoying the contrast of sunlight and shadows, bare trunks and pine needles against a dropcloth of snow. Again, he wished he had his camera.

"You must wish you had your camera," Jayne echoed, coming to stand beside him. "This is supposed to be one of the most beautiful parts of Hawkridge."

"Supposed to be?"

She folded her arms, gripping her elbows with her hands. "I don't spend much time here—I'm not very comfortable in the woods. I like the open lawns much better, especially in the snow."

"You have your fair share of quirks, don't you?"

She lifted her chin. "No more than anyone else."

He dismissed her defensive answer with a wave of his hand. "Especially for someone who works with troubled girls, trying to help them adjust."

Her fists clenched and she let her arms fall to her sides. "Are you implying that I'm unfit to take care of the students?"

"Not at all." A call from farther along the path summoned them to the "perfect" tree. "Everybody has problems. I think you ignore yours." Without waiting for a response, he walked toward the cluster of girls.

"It's The Tree," Haley announced as he reached them. "We all agree." They'd used their hands to pull the snow away from its base, revealing the trunk.

Chris tilted his head. "Well, it's not too tall, but tall enough." Seven nods ratified his judgment. "A little too thin, do you think?"

The girls disagreed. "It's slender."

"Graceful."

"Elegant."

"Spiritual."

He held up a hand. "Got it. Well, if this is your choice, then I'll start chopping. Everybody step ten paces backward without bumping into anything."

When the girls were at a safe distance, Chris grasped the ax handle, then brought the heavy head back to his shoulder. He took a breath, lifted his elbows and rotated his hips as he started the arc of the cut. The blade swung within an inch of his cheekbone, taking on a momentum of its own.

A voice cried, "No! Wait!"

Chris couldn't stop the swing. But he managed to bury the blade in the snow and dirt in front of the tree, slicing off a few branch tips in the process. And not, luckily, his toes.

He rounded on the girls. "Who the hell yelled at me? Are you crazy?"

Jayne stepped in front of him, blocking his view of the guilty party. "Never use that tone with my students. Do you understand?"

He'd meant to apologize. Instead, he glared back at her. "A trick like that could have cost me a leg."

"It wasn't a trick."

"Just a damn stupid thing to do."

"Watch your language."

"I'll say what I please."

Sarah's soft voice entered the tense silence. "I'm sorry, Mr. Hammond. I thought we should ask Ms. Thomas if this tree would be okay. Before you cut it down."

As his heart rate slowed, his temper cooled. He took a step backward, physically and mentally. "And I'm sorry I yelled, Sarah. But for a second there, I saw my toes hopping off in all different directions."

Jayne blew out a short breath that sounded like a snort. "Excellent. Everyone has apologized. And that tree is fine.

Now, the rest of you can go off in twos or threes to gather whatever else you want. I brought along clippers and plastic bags. Let's leave Mr. Hammond…to his chopping." She said his name in a crisp tone.

The crowd dispersed, with Jayne following. Chris cut down the tree with a few strategic blows and pulled it trunk first to the trail for the hike back. From his slight uphill position he could see three groups of girls in bright-colored coats inspecting holly trees, cedars and pines for the greenery they wanted. The one person he couldn't see was their fearless—or not so fearless but certainly gutsy—leader.

"Look, mistletoe!"

He glanced over to where Haley pointed up into the bare branches above their heads. No one would be able to climb that high. When he reached them, he said so.

"I like climbing tress," Haley insisted. "I could do it."

"With a sprained wrist?" Chris nodded at the sling she'd been taking advantage of to get out of chores.

"Well…" He could see her thinking quickly. "I guess not." She gasped and looked at Chris. "You can climb trees, can't you?"

"Not that high."

Taryn took up her friend's cause. "Oh, please. Mistletoe is so important to us pagans!"

Frowning, he shook his head. "Find some closer to the ground." Then he went back to the trail to find Jayne.

The snow wasn't as deep under the trees as on the bare lawn, but moving around still took effort. Jayne's track lay ahead of him—the deep wells of her steps and between them the shallower brush of each foot, pushing aside the snow. She'd followed the trail, more or less, though occasionally she'd wandered to one side or the other, once where a perfectly circular bird's nest had fallen out of the tree above, and another time where a spray of golden autumn leaves still shivered on a small branch.

Then she'd veered from the path altogether, wandering down a steeper slope, through a grove of hardwood trees growing close together, their trunks forming straight black lines between snow and sky.

Pausing at the edge of the grove, he called again, at the top of his voice. "Jayne? Jayne, what the hell are you doing?"

She didn't answer and he forged on, seriously worried.

The girls heard his shout and came to join him.

Beth arrived first. "Where's Tommy?"

"Ms. Thomas wouldn't wander away in the snow," Sarah fretted.

"She hates snow."

"Yeah. She doesn't like the woods, either."

"Yeah."

"Is she okay, Mr. Hammond? Have you found her?"

"No." Reclaiming those climbing skills from the past, he crawled onto the wide trunk of a nearby fallen tree to get a wider view. "Wait. What's that?" Dark blue cloth and a streak of mahogany hair lay farther down the hill. He called Jayne's name again, but got no answer.

Back down in the snow again, he pinned each girl with his fiercest stare. "Do not. Leave. This place. I can't rescue all of you."

Sarah stepped forward from the group. "We won't follow or turn back. We'll stay right here. Go get her."

He descended the slope as fast as he could, stumbling, falling several times, dodging trees and stumps and fighting the suffocating snow. "Jayne?"

There she was, lying facedown beside a huge tree stump

on the opposite edge of a slight depression. Chris tried to hurry, tried to keep his head up, his eyes on Jayne.

But his foot caught and he fell forward, stretching his arms out, expecting a faceful of the white stuff.

Instead he dropped through the snow, and into a thick tunnel of thorn bushes underneath. The skin of his face tore going in, and tore again in different places as he reared up.

"Jayne!" She was less than ten feet away.

Her arm moved and she turned her head to the side.

Then he saw the bloody snow.

He floundered through the ditch they'd both tripped into, and sank to his knees beside her. Her face was turned away from him.

"Don't move, honey, don't move." He panted, unable to catch his breath. "Just lie still. Let me check you out." Stripping off his gloves, he felt over her arms and legs and slipped a cold bare hand under her jacket to explore her ribs and shoulders. "Can you feel your feet? Your fingers?"

She wiggled her fingers and flexed her feet as an answer.

"Knees? Elbows?" Her limbs seemed to work. "Okay, honey, I'm going to put my hand at the back of your neck. Can you roll to your side? I'll help you—just push yourself over. Good."

Lying on her side, she curled her arms into her chest and groaned. He gave her several minutes to recover.

"Now, honey, I'd like you to roll the rest of the way over. Don't work too hard. I've got your head in my hand. Yeah, that's right…just sink backward." Still cradling her arms to her chest, she eased onto her back.

"Oh, Jesus," Chris breathed. "You hit your face, sweetheart. Right on that big fat stump."

"I did?" She'd kept her eyes closed since help arrived, but now she lifted her lids, trying to see. Black fog hovered at the edges of her vision as she focused on the man bending over her. Did she know him? Loose, waving brown hair, bright blue eyes, that sexy mouth—

"Chris?" Surging up, she grabbed his shoulders, making sure he was real. "Chris, are you okay? What happened? We started sliding and then the headlights pointed down...I heard trees breaking. Where's the car?" She broke free of his gaze and looked around, then back into his face. "I don't understand. Where are we? What's going on?"

"Juliet?" he said in a strangled voice.

A black tide poured into her head. She couldn't see, couldn't hear or feel. She sagged to the side, as everything started to spin....

Hands took hold of her. A man said, "I've got you."

Suddenly, her vision returned. Her eyes were open and she could see Chris Hammond leaning over her with panic in his eyes.

Jayne blinked hard. "Chris? What's happened?" He protested, but she ignored him and sat up, putting her back against the tree stump she'd seen just before she hit it. Her face ached. "That's right—I tripped, and I couldn't stop the fall. I must look awful."

She pressed gentle fingers to her forehead and nose, feeling a wide expanse of broken skin and swelling. "Oh, I am a mess." Scooping up some of the damn snow in both hands, she cupped it against her injuries. "Are the girls okay?"

"They're fine." His voice still sounded strained.

"Is there anything I can do to look less frightening?"

"Don't think so."

Jayne laid her hands in her lap and took a good look at Chris's face. "You're all cut up, too. I'm so sorry."

He drew a deep breath and sat back on his haunches. "Why

did you leave the trail? What in the world are you doing this far into the woods?"

Using her hands and feet, Jayne moved backward and up, so she could sit on the stump's flat top. She didn't want to think about those confusing minutes on the trail, the echoes of her dreams, the feeling that she'd been there before.

"I heard Taryn say she wanted mistletoe. I thought I saw some close to the ground." She tried to twist at the waist to point out her find, and got a taste of how sore her muscles were going to be. "Ow. It's there." She cocked a thumb over her shoulder. "Behind me."

Chris's gaze didn't search out the mistletoe. "You must have hit your head pretty hard. What do you remember after you fell?"

"Um...nothing," Jayne realized with surprise. "I saw the mistletoe and took a step toward it, then I was falling...and just now I woke up."

His eyes narrowed. "You remember waking up?"

"With you leaning over me." When he continued to stare at her, she frowned at him. "What's wrong? Did something else happen?"

He drew a deep breath, then blew it out again. "No. Nothing. I guess." He put both hands on one knee and straightened up, then reached out to her. "We'd better get back to the girls. I told them not to move from that spot and Sarah promised they wouldn't."

Jayne gave him her hand and he started pulling her to her feet. But when her full weight came to bear on her right leg, she gasped and sat down again. "I think I hurt my knee. Why don't you bring them here so they can get the mistletoe? Maybe by then I'll feel like walking home."

Chris started to say something, then turned to go back to

the trail. In a few minutes the girls surrounded Jayne, exclaiming over her face. When she told them about the mistletoe, Haley and Monique trudged off and returned with a bagful.

"Very good." Jayne smiled and stood up from the tree trunk, pretending the simple move didn't hurt like hell. "Let's get back to the manor. It's time for lunch. Be very careful walking up to the trail. We don't want any more falls."

The girls, young and graceful, gamboled through the woods like puppies, falling and getting up with no trouble at all. Jayne followed as fast as she could, but her knee had stiffened, her whole head throbbed with pain and her right eye was swollen almost shut.

She looked at Chris, walking beside her. "I'm getting a black eye, aren't I?"

He nodded. "A doozy."

"Wonderful." They reached the edge of the trail and she stopped to lean against a convenient tree. "What are you upset about?"

"Me? Nothing." But he wouldn't meet her eyes with his own.

"Did I say something I don't remember when I was waking up?" Surely she hadn't told him she cared about him, or even that she thought she was falling in love with him. That would be so foolish…so futile.

"Nothing important." He turned toward the top of the trail, where the girls waited beside their tree. "Do you need some help?"

"No, thanks." She straightened up, swallowing a groan. "I can make it."

But pride only got her so far on her own. The trail wasn't steep, but as her bruises woke up, as her knee began to swell and her cuts to burn, she began to wonder if she could manage the rest of the journey back.

Chris had left her to walk at the front of their little Yule procession, carrying the heavy end of the tree. When Jayne stopped for the fourth or fifth time, however, he called Sarah and Monique to help Selena and Haley with the tree, telling them to go ahead with the other three girls.

Then he walked back to where Jayne stood. "Sure you don't need some help?" His tone was brusque, but his eyes were kind.

"Maybe," she admitted. "I didn't remember coming this far."

He put his arm around her back, with his hand firmly tucked beneath her arm. "Sometimes the way home seems to take forever."

Jayne only nodded, as she stepped down again on her bad knee. They didn't talk again for the rest of the hike. She discovered walking was easier if she wrapped her arm around Chris's waist, too, allowing him to carry a little more of her weight on that bad side. He took a firmer hold in his turn, and even through her many layers of clothes she could feel the pressure of his fingers on the side of her breast. If her heart hadn't already been pounding from exertion, his touch would have jump-started the engine.

By the time she hobbled into the building, the girls had shed their snow clothes in the storeroom and wanted to hover around as she shed hers.

"I'm fine," she assured them. Then she looked at the jumble of outerwear on the floor. "This room, however, is not. Please hang up your coats and scarves and spread your gloves and hats on the table to dry. Finally, take your boots and knock the snow off of them outside before you set them in the hallway near the door."

Grumbling, they followed her orders, giving Jayne a chance to peel off her outer layers in relative privacy. The building felt colder to her than before, which she chalked up to reaction. A cup of tea would solve the problem.

But an hour later, bundled into a blanket and snuggled into the corner of the sofa closest to the fire, with a mug of tea half-finished, she had to admit she still felt chilled. The off-and-on dizziness and blurred vision she kept to herself.

Chris sat on the arm of the sofa, peering into her face, his fingers moving gently over the line of her jaw. "I'd bet you're in shock. Who knows how long you were unconscious before I got there?"

"Not long, I'm sure." She brushed his hand away, because she couldn't be sure her reaction would remain hidden. "I'll be okay if I stay warm for a while. Would you mind building up the fire?"

"No." His tone and sharp movements conveyed irritation.

With all the girls in the kitchen making lunch, she felt it safe to ask, "What have I done this time?"

He jammed another log into the blaze. "Besides nearly killing yourself?"

"Not intentionally, I assure you."

The logs shifted as he stabbed the poker between them. Flames shot up the chimney and heat gusted across the room. "I get tired of being pushed away. You wouldn't even let me clean up those scrapes on your face."

"Why would you expect anything else?"

"Because…" He ran a hand through his hair, but didn't finish the sentence.

"We're not really friends, are we?" Jayne squeezed her eyes shut against the spinning in her head. "We've only known each other a few days."

"What difference does that make?

The question stunned her, and she stared at him with her

mouth open. Was he implying…had he begun to think about her as someone beside Juliet?

"Lunchtime!" Selena sang out from the doorway. She came in carrying a tray for Jayne—cold cheese sandwiches, chips and soda. The rest of the girls followed with their own plates, plus one for Chris, who retreated to his chair by the fireplace. Over these last days each girl had claimed a space of her own. Haley sat on the end of the other sofa, closest to the fire, with Taryn beside her and Yolanda by the other arm. Beth and Selena occupied the two armchairs facing that couch, while Monique and Sarah filled the other sofa with Jayne. After the strenuous morning, they ate in silence for a few minutes because even dull food tasted good when you were hungry.

Then Haley sighed, holding up half her sandwich and staring at it. "I wish this was a piece of sausage pizza."

"Mmm."

"That sounds so good."

"I'd wish for black olives and mushrooms," Beth said.

Jayne was quite proud when no one insulted that choice.

Monique added her own favorite, instead. "Spinach and garlic for me."

After another pause, Taryn said, "I wish Mr. Hammond would go on with the story."

Amid the chorus of agreement, someone asked, "What other kinds of adventures did Chase and Juliet have?"

Chris looked at Jayne for permission. She gave him a slight nod, hoping her obvious hesitation would persuade him to refuse.

But either her signal was too weak or he chose to misunderstand the message. "Okay," he said, settling back with his mug of hot chocolate. "I'll keep it short, though, because you've got other things to do."

Jayne decided she would be forgiven if she slept through

the afternoon's installment. When Monique and Sarah moved down to stretch out on the carpet, Jayne put her legs up on the sofa, hoping to ease some of the aches in her shoulders and back. She was vaguely aware that one of the girls tucked a soft pillow under her head. Another blanket fell over her.

With her eyes closed, the blurred vision didn't matter, and the dizziness eased. The shivering subsided as she started to warm up. She was thrilled to be so sleepy…to be falling asleep….

Chris told the girls some of the funnier anecdotes from his adventures with Juliet over the years—the summer trail ride during which his horse had deliberately run him into a tree branch and knocked him flat on his back; the winter afternoon they'd outskied a small avalanche; the Christmas Day they'd volunteered to cook dinner for Charlie and almost burned the cabin down.

What Chris didn't detail was the ripening physical relationship they experienced. These girls didn't need to hear how kisses matured, how one touch kindled the need for more, how resolutions were made only to be broken. He'd preserved Juliet's virginity for her, whether she appreciated the effort or not.

But only just. And only until she was seventeen.

For the rest of the afternoon, however, he suggested the girls work on the decorations for their holiday. Since glue seemed to be involved, he pointed out that the tile-topped kitchen table would be easier to clean than the polished antique ones in the library.

He was pretty proud of himself for the idea, since now Jayne could sleep in peace, without the voices of the girls disturbing the rest she sorely needed. He planted himself in the armchair closest to the library door, in case anyone tried to wake her. Or glued their fingers together and needed help.

Since he hadn't been getting much rest himself—in a frigid

room on a hard bed, troubled by dreams of Juliet when he did sleep and haunted by memories of making love with Jayne when he lay awake in the dark—only a few minutes passed before his eyelids drifted down.

Just a little while, he told himself, easing his head into the corner of the chair's soft cushion. *Only a short nap.*

Next thing he knew, he was on his feet, eyes wide open.

Jayne had started screaming.

Chapter Ten

Chris was beside her in a second. The girls arrived a moment later.

"Jayne, honey, wake up." As he took hold of her shoulders, she started to fight, slapping at his arms, hitting his chest with her fists.

"No, no. Please..." She was crying now, more than screaming, and cowering in the corner of the sofa. "Don't."

"Jayne, stop it." He gave her a sharp shake, made his voice equally sharp. "You're scaring the girls."

She froze, and turned her face out of the pillow. "Girls...what girls? I don't remember..." The tears started again.

As she had stared at him, though, Chris thought her gaze seemed...different. Not just confused and terrified, but...well, the only word that occurred to him was *young*. She'd had that same expression out in the woods, when he'd have sworn she remembered who she was.

He glanced at Sarah and the rest of the students, standing speechless at the sight of their headmistress in total panic.

"You all should go back into the kitchen," he told them gently. "Figure out what we can pull together for supper." They hesitated, and he tried for more concrete directions, like

Jayne's would be. "See if you can find some hot dogs—we could cook on sticks over the fire."

Once Sarah had shooed the last of the girls across the hall, Chris left the couch long enough to close the library door. When he turned around, he saw immediately that a different woman now confronted him.

Jayne had straightened up, smoothed her wrinkled sweater and the blanket, and fluffed the pillows at her side. She'd removed the band holding her hair, combed her fingers through the tangles, and was in the process of restoring her ponytail when he sat down in front of her on the coffee table.

"Your hair is beautiful," he said quietly. "Why not wear it loose?"

"It's always in the way." A thread of unease ran through the pragmatic answer. With her hair fixed, her clothes neater and her hands gripped together in her lap, she met his eyes. "What just happened? What did I do?"

"You woke up screaming. And crying."

"Oh, my God." She covered her face with her hands. "The girls must be distraught."

"What about you? Do you remember the dream? Do you remember waking up?"

Jayne kept her face hidden as she struggled with the question. If she told him about the dreams, the confusion and the fear, would he use them against her? Would he insist she was discovering her "real" self—Juliet Radcliffe?

Could he be right?

"I saw trees." She took a deep breath, letting her hands fall into her lap, but keeping her eyes closed. "All kinds of evergreens, thousands of them. No snow on the ground, just dark earth and that piney, woodsy smell.

"Then there was only one tree, not in the woods but in a room with mirrors on the walls, and a shiny dark floor. The tree was decorated for Christmas, with white lights and silver icicles."

"Okay." Chris leaned forward to take her hands in his. "What else?"

"I—I'm not sure. I was waiting for…something. Something I'm afraid of. I can't find a door or a window, can't get away. All I can do is sit and wait." She opened her eyes to look at him. "That's all."

"That was the dream?" When she nodded, he asked, "Was waking up still part of the dream?"

"Maybe." Jayne pulled her hands free to massage her eyes with her fingers. "I—I've had these moments when I wasn't…well, *oriented* is the technical term. For a few seconds, I feel as if I'm somewhere else."

"This afternoon on the path?"

Jayne shrugged. "A couple of other times, too. And the strange dreams."

She waited for him to take advantage of her confession, but he sat without speaking, staring at the floor between them, for a long time.

"I don't recall much about my life," she found herself saying into the silence. "I remember things my grandmother told me about my family, my childhood. But when I try to search for—for my own memories, I come up against a barrier, like a blank wall."

Chris got to his feet and went to put more logs on the fire. "Does this wall exist at a particular point in time? Does it have a before and after? For instance, do you remember last week?"

"Of course."

"Last year?"

"Yes."

"Ten years ago?"

"Ten years ago, I was a freshman in college. That was just after my grandmother died."

"How old were you then?"

"Twenty. I started later than usual," she explained, before he could ask. "I developed meningitis when I was eighteen, and nearly died. It took me a couple of years to recover enough to go to school."

"You remember being sick?"

"I remember waking up from the coma with my grandmother by the bed."

"In a hospital?"

"In her house. They had sent me home to die, she said. That I woke up at all was a miracle."

"Ah." He turned back to the fire, pushing the logs around with the poker even though the blaze was going well.

"What does 'Ah' mean? What are you thinking?" When he didn't answer, she forced her stiff and aching self off the sofa and went to stand beside him. "It's my brain. My life. What should I know?"

Still, he didn't look at her. "I'm not sure. You had a bad fall this afternoon—that's enough to be worried about. You've been under a lot of stress. I think...I think you should let this go until we get out of here. Then maybe you can talk to somebody about what's going on."

"'Somebody' as in a therapist? Doctors?"

He shrugged both shoulders, and winced. "Maybe."

"You don't get to be a therapist without taking therapy, Chris. None of this came up in my training."

"Maybe you needed—what's the word?—a catalyst."

"You?"

This time he shrugged only the good shoulder.

She grabbed the arm with the poker to keep it still. "You've been pushing me for days to remember something I don't. Now, suddenly, you want me to get counseling? When the snow melts?"

Without shaking off her grasp, he returned the poker to the stand. Then he faced her directly and cupped his hands around her upper arms.

"You're right. I barreled in here thinking I knew what was going on. But..." He pulled in a deep breath. "Things are much more complicated than I realized. I don't think there's an easy answer anymore. Or even a right answer."

He lifted a hand to run his fingers lightly over her scraped forehead, along her temple and the line of her jaw. After hesitating a second at the point of her chin, he brushed the pad of his thumb over her lips.

His blue gaze met Jayne's. "We have a HanYuleMasZa celebration to endure and seven girls to entertain until the power comes on. I'm willing to let the problems of the past rest for now. If you can."

He'd conceded the battle. She wouldn't have to defend herself any longer. Chris was willing to accept her as Jayne, not Juliet. And he touched her as if Jayne meant something to him. As if Jayne was the woman he wanted.

But the questions he'd asked, the discrepancies he'd forced her to acknowledge, couldn't be ignored. Jayne realized she needed to discover the truth about herself and her life. Somehow the present and the past would have to be reconciled before she could be sure of who she was.

But not right now. "I can do that," she assured him, with a slight smile. "Something to eat and a good night's sleep seem like enough to manage for one night."

"Don't forget KwanChrisHanYule." He grinned at her.

She sighed. "I only wish I could."

AFTER A DINNER of skewered hot dogs followed by s'mores for dessert, the girls worked awhile longer on their holiday preparations, but none of them required the least prompting to change into pajamas and settle in the library for an early bedtime.

Chris had no intention of continuing his story tonight, even when the usual requests for more started. "Let's take a break," he suggested. "I'd like to hear some of your stories."

From Monique's loud, "No way," to Sarah's doubtful frown, they all rejected that idea.

"Not the bad stuff. You must have had some good times in your lives. Can you think of one to talk about?"

When he glanced at Jayne, the expression on her face knocked the breath out of him. That smile, the one he'd wanted to see, beamed at him from across the room. He read pride in her gaze, affection and maybe love. At least she loved what he'd just done. That was a great step toward the real thing.

Before they turned their flashlights off, each girl told a story of her own. Monique had them all cheering her play-by-play basketball win. Taryn told about a séance where she'd spoken to her dead grandmother, and none of the girls expressed the least doubt. Beth's Bat Mitzvah disaster story made everyone laugh. Selena talked about finding a stranded whale on a California beach, and the girls cried when they learned the animal couldn't be saved. Chris had to blink his eyes a couple of times to see clearly after that one.

Haley gave them a funny account of her first ice-skating lesson at Rockefeller Center in New York. Yolanda described watermelon seed spitting contests in Baton Rouge in the summertime and the ribbons she won each year.

Sarah's turn came. She paused for a few seconds, then

said, "My story is about how I got stranded in the middle of a blizzard with six people I didn't like very much."

The girls around her stirred. Several of them glanced at Jayne in protest.

But the headmistress kept her gaze on Sarah and didn't lose the smile she'd been wearing when the last story ended.

"From what I knew of them," Sarah continued, "they were all hard to get along with. One of them was just a brat, a weird new girl who couldn't get along with anybody. The Jewish girl was always bragging about how rich she was and how she could have anything she wanted."

Taryn had buried her face in her pink bunny. Beth burrowed into her sleeping bag and turned her back on everyone.

"The two black girls acted like everybody else was putting them down because of their race, when really people didn't want to be with them because they just didn't cooperate. The girl from California acted pretty much the same, in Spanish. And the girl from New York thought everybody else was stupid because they hadn't grown up in 'The City.'"

Now even Chris looked to Jayne for intervention, because the big library suddenly felt like the interior of an iceberg.

"But the most amazing thing happened when the power failed." Sarah hugged her knees to her chest. "Suddenly, we were in trouble. No heat, no lights, no way to cook except over the fire. There was some complaining at first, some arguments.

"But gradually, everyone started to cooperate. Nobody cared much where they'd come from anymore, or what problems brought them here. What mattered was being able to take care of ourselves...and each other. We all wanted to be warm, we all wanted to eat. So we all started doing what had to be done. Together."

She looked at each of the other girls in turn, even to the point of getting up and walking over to kneel in front of Beth.

"So from now on, whenever somebody asks me to think about the good times in my life, the memories I want to keep forever, this week will be at the top of my list. The week when I learned how to love every single one of the girls I thought I didn't like."

Chris found himself blinking his eyes again, especially when all of the girls piled on top of each other in an effort to share hugs. A long time passed before they all felt satisfied they'd given and received enough love.

Sarah stood up again. "Something else I learned this week—what being an adult and taking responsibility really means. I hope I can face tough situations with the same strength and kindness and imagination that Ms. Thomas and Mr. Hammond have shown us this week."

All the girls rose then, and gave a standing ovation. Jayne let her tears show but, being a guy, Chris blinked his back. He couldn't remember the last time he'd cried so often.

Then he realized he *could* remember when he'd cried like this. But he didn't want to think about the past tonight.

So he grinned at their applause and said thanks, then went outside to bring in more logs. He stood for a while by the woodpile, hoping the girls would be asleep by the time he went back. And he noticed a change in the air, a softness that predicted warmer temperatures and melting snow.

Even Jayne had fallen asleep when he returned to the library. He set his logs down as quietly as possible and fed the fire to be sure they'd be warm all night.

Then, because he thought he'd earned it, Chris settled into one of the armchairs. With his feet stretched out on the ottoman and his head wedged at just the right angle into the soft corner, he closed his eyes and spent the night with seven girls. And one woman.

Which was why they were all awakened the next morning by the sound of someone knocking on the glass panes of Emmeline's garden doors.

"I CAN'T BELIEVE YOU'VE been trapped up here for four days without power." Steve Greeley shook his head and took another gulp of coffee. "Drinking only instant coffee."

The deputy grinned at Jayne and she was forced to smile back, though every cut and bruise on her face protested. "We've been pretty comfortable, overall. The fireplace made all the difference, of course."

Steve had driven his snowmobile from town to check on Jayne and the girls, as promised. Ron Pruitt, another member of the Ridgeville sheriff's department, had come with Steve on his own snowmobile. She and Chris had brought the men into the kitchen, where the girls had made an appearance before asking if they could go back to bed and get warm again.

"Having somebody who knows how to cook on the fire must've helped." Ron commented. "Not many people have that skill anymore."

Jayne nodded, pretending to sip her coffee. The truth was, she didn't know what she'd done in her childhood. Listening to the girls' stories last night had demonstrated exactly how little she remembered of her own life.

"It's too bad you got hurt, though." Steve studied her face, which the mirror had already told her looked like a mask from the latest horror film. "I think you should see a doctor. Right away. And the girl with the hurt wrist needs to go down with us, too."

A glance at Chris showed him completely outside the conversation. He sat back in his chair at the kitchen table, drinking his coffee and looking as if his thoughts were a thousand miles away. With his background, they probably were.

She turned back to Steve. "I agree that Haley should have her wrist examined. We've kept snow on it, but there's no question that it's still swollen. I can't leave, however. At least, not unless all the girls can go, too."

"Well, we can't carry seven girls plus you and…" His wary look at Chris reminded Jayne of two dogs in the presence of a single bone. "…and Mr. Hammond, here. The weather's warming up, though. Couple of days, this snow will really start to disappear. Joe Garber told me he'd have the highway plowed up this far by late tomorrow afternoon."

"The school has a contract with the county to plow our drive, as well. Did he mention that?"

Steve scratched his head. "Uh…no. I'll have to remind him."

"I'd appreciate it. Now, what about the electricity? Has power been restored to Ridgeville?"

He pulled a big frown. "Should happen in the next day or so. Big transformer got taken out by a tree—huge sucker, and the power company needed this long to get it cut up and hauled away so they could reach the wires. I saw at least five downed lines on the way up here. I'd say it'll be several days, if not weeks, before you get power this far into the mountains."

Jayne fell back in her chair. This was not what she wanted to hear.

"Have you checked on everybody in town?" Chris spoke for the first time. "My granddad lives out River Road. Has anybody been there?"

Ron chuckled. "We didn't get out there before he got into the office in town, raising he— Uh, raising Cain about you heading up here and not coming back. Feisty old geezer."

Chris blew out a deep breath. "Feisty. That's Charlie."

After slurping the rest of his coffee, Steve got to his feet. "Okay, Ms. Thomas, I think we should get you and that student of yours down to the doctor. We each can take one of you."

Jayne stood, too, careful to keep weight off her injured knee and trying to ignore the stiffness in every other muscle.

"I can't leave, Steve. There are six other girls here."

"Hammond can—"

"No, he can't. I am responsible for these students. I can't leave them in someone else's care."

His eyes narrowed, but he nodded. "Okay, if you insist. We'll take the girl, I guess."

"And do what with her, once she's seen the doctor? She's with me because she couldn't go home. Her parents aren't in Ridgeville. You would have to bring her back."

"Oh, yeah." He thought for a minute, then brightened. "We'll take you both down and bring you both back." Before Jayne could correct him, he found the answer himself. "But that leaves the other girls here with Hammond."

Then he grinned. "So we'll just take him back with us." He turned to the man in question. "You can check on your granddad yourself."

Jayne stared at Chris, and after a moment he lifted his gaze to stare back. As much as she hadn't wanted him to stay at the beginning, she didn't want him to leave now. They—the girls and she—needed him.

But perhaps he needed to go. If he'd come to Ridgeville to see Charlie, then he was wasting time he wouldn't get back.

"Maybe you should—" she began.

"I can't—" he said at the same time.

They both stopped. Then Jayne, being selfish, motioned for Chris to continue.

He gave her a half smile, then looked at Steve. "Jayne should see a doctor, but you're not going to get her away from these girls without dynamite. There are…liability issues involved, you know."

From his furrowed forehead, Jayne thought perhaps Steve didn't know.

"If I leave," Chris said, "Jayne will have sole responsibility for seven lively kids. She's not in any shape to carry wood, stoke the fire or deal with urgent repairs that might come up. I think the students and Jayne will all be safer if I stay."

"But—" Steve began.

"Since Jayne can't leave, I think Haley should stay with us. Her wrist will wait another couple of days. Maybe you could point out to the snowplow guy that there's an injured kid up here who needs help. That should be incentive. And I'll give you a note for Charlie."

Jayne almost laughed aloud at Steve's frustrated expression. Instead she put a hand on his arm and marshaled a grateful smile. "I appreciate the effort you made to check on us. That's above and beyond the call of duty, I think."

Now both deputies blushed bright red.

"If you don't mind, I'll give you a list of phone numbers for the girls' parents. If you would call them all and reassure them that we're fine and will be down in town as soon as the roads are clear, I would be even more grateful."

She gave Steve the list and then, using her headmistress experience, talked the deputies into their coats and walked them down the hallway to the outside door where they'd parked their snowmobiles.

As Steve stopped to protest once more, Jayne leaned up and kissed his cheek. "Thank you so much," she said in a low voice. "Have a safe trip back." She squeezed his arm and, at the same time, urged him out of the building.

Standing in the doorway, she waved as they gunned their engines, and again as they wheeled around before disappearing down the drive.

When she shut herself inside, she found Chris standing in the hallway, arms crossed over his chest, his handsome face marred with a scowl. "Was the kiss necessary?"

There was, Jayne thought, a distinct tint of green in those blue eyes. She managed a small, flirtatious shrug. "It's all he gets." Then she stepped past Chris and went to see if the girls planned to spend the entire day in their pajamas.

WITH THEIR CLOTHES changed, the girls started serious work on their holiday decorating. Chris devised a stand for the tree using a cleaning bucket and bricks to keep it upright. Since the ornaments would be paper, greenery and pinecones, the tree branches wouldn't have to bear much weight. After an intense bargaining session, the tree was placed in the center of the library underneath the double-tiered brass chandelier.

"I like it better that way," he told Jayne as he set up a ladder beside the tree. "I can tie the top to the chandelier and be sure the tree stays standing."

"As long as the chandelier isn't damaged." She stood with her hands gripped together and the line between her brows telegraphing worry.

"So I can fall flat on the floor and break every bone in my body, as long as there's not a scratch on the brass, is that what you're saying?"

She recognized the teasing and smiled at him. "Exactly."

He nodded. "Good to know." And good to have this kind of harmony, this sense of partnership and trust. They'd come together to chase the nosy deputies back to town. Not literally, of course, but with a shared, though unspoken, understanding that they must protect the group—the *family*—from the threat of intrusion.

Not for much longer, though. The snow was softening, the temperatures inching higher, and in a day, maybe two, the outside world would invade again.

He tied the tree top to the chandelier with the skeins of dark green wool Jayne had given him. "This yarn is so soft, the chandelier won't feel a thing," he assured her.

"That's mohair," she said. "It had better be soft, as expensive as it is." Then she chuckled. "I bought it the day you were chasing me all over town."

"Stalking you." Jayne steadied the ladder as he backed down. And she didn't move away when he reached the floor, so they were standing close together. He put a hand on her shoulder. "I owe you an apology for that."

She shook her head, but her smile faded. "Clearly, there's something I don't know about myself. But…" She raised her troubled golden gaze to his. "…if I was here when I was younger, why doesn't anyone else recognize me?"

Chris had thought about that. "Most people see what they expect to see. No one in town would be looking for Juliet." He took a deep breath. "Except me. I never stopped thinking about her. Wanting her, looking for her even when I knew she was dead."

He'd said the wrong thing. Jayne's face changed suddenly, even as the girls' voices sounded in the hallway.

"Oh, look, it's ready!"

"Wow, cool!"

They came streaming into the library. Jayne stepped back from him, and then away. She'd restored her headmistress expression—patient, friendly, but also wary. "It is a beautiful tree," she said as they all gathered around. "I can't wait to see your ornaments!"

Chapter Eleven

She rarely lied to her students, but Jayne told a huge lie in that moment. She didn't want to see the tree decorated, wasn't in the least enthusiastic about watching the library transformed into a holiday setting. With every step they took along this path, her uneasiness increased.

As if that weren't enough, Chris had just confirmed her worst fears. He still thought of her as Juliet.

Perhaps she had been, once upon a time. With all the missing pieces in her memory, she couldn't deny the possibility. And she couldn't begin to explain why she would have let Chris believe she was dead. Obviously, she hadn't remembered him. She still didn't. Why not?

Chris hadn't told her how Juliet "died," except to say he'd thought for twelve years that he'd killed her. Dead people usually left a body behind. Why assume she was dead, if there wasn't a corpse?

Perhaps, after all, this was simply a case of a strong likeness between Jayne and Juliet. The same hair and skin, the same eye color—these things happened all the time. Chris had never seen the birthmark on Jayne's hip, so he couldn't know without a doubt that Juliet's looked identical. Logic and reason suggested a genetic resemblance. That was all.

Even if Jayne had been Juliet, she wasn't anymore. She didn't remember a background of money and status; true or not, she recalled a middle class family and upbringing. Her adult self had been shaped by those memories and her years with Elizabeth Jayne Thomas, not by anything that had happened to Juliet. So the person she had become was not the person Juliet might have been.

By his own admission, the woman Chris had responded to in these last few days was not the woman Jayne knew herself to be. The disappointment struck her like an arrow to the heart.

She had fallen in love with the Chris Hammond she'd come to know. He was simply glad to have rediscovered the Juliet he'd loved twelve years ago.

Fortunately, Jayne had her responsibility to the girls to fall back on. The preparations in the library consumed the entire day, with a break for chili cooked over the fire at lunch. Yolanda and Monique worked with Jayne in the kitchen on the holiday meal. With the exception of sherry wine or liqueur, the ingredients for a traditional English trifle were easy to find—cake from the freezer, rich raspberry jam and canned peaches, instant pudding and whipping cream. Jayne would have omitted the sherry in any case.

Both Monique and Yolanda contributed to whipping the cream. "This is taking forever," Monique complained after a minute spent whisking. "How long do we have to beat this stuff, anyway?"

Yolanda lasted about two minutes. "Man, my wrist is tired." By taking turns, the two girls managed to froth the cream into thick, stiff peaks. And when Jayne covered the top of the trifle with those peaks, the two girls stood back in awe.

"Looks beautiful." Monique brushed a finger through the leftover cream in the bowl.

"And delicious." Yolanda licked the spoon. "I can't wait to get a big helping."

"First," Jayne reminded them, "we have chickens to roast and potatoes to bake."

Yet another of the antique cooking tools kept on display in the main kitchen was a roasting spit, which Chris installed in the library fireplace. An iron rod speared the three chickens neck to tail and was then suspended over a bed of coals to cook the meat. Monique assumed responsibility for turning the spit every half hour to keep the birds cooking evenly.

Yolanda went back to the kitchen with Jayne. Together they wrapped ten potatoes in aluminum foil to be placed on the coals for baking. Then they peeled oranges and bananas to create a fruit salad called ambrosia, and prepared green beans to be cooked in a pot over the fire.

"This looks as good as any meal I ever had." Yolanda was stirring coconut in with the oranges and bananas. "You really know how to cook, Ms. Thomas."

Jayne shook her head. "I'm just making do with what we have. Thank goodness for the boxed dressing mix and the canned cranberry sauce."

About four o'clock, as the daylight began to wane through the windows, Taryn and Haley came into the kitchen.

"Can we set the table?" Taryn carried a bag of holly with her. "Is it okay if we use candles tonight?"

"That will be nice." Jayne tried to decide where to hide next, since the holiday had now invaded her kitchen as well as the library. "Since we're going to be elegant, I think I'll get into some different clothes."

She stopped in the library to tell Monique where she would be, in case something happened with the chickens. The meat seemed to be progressing nicely, however.

"You go," Monique told her. "Take your time. We're all good."

Jayne paused in the doorway to watch Chris hanging a pine branch garland across one of the windows. He was concentrating, while listening to instructions from three different girls, and so didn't look her way.

Which was just as well. She couldn't afford to lose—as one of her favorite songs put it so well—another piece of her heart.

DINNERTIME HAD BEEN SET for five o'clock. Chris assembled with the girls in the big entry hall at four fifty-five to wait for the headmistress. Then they would all process together to the kitchen, where dinner waited on the table. After dinner, the library would be revealed.

The girls had changed into party colors. They all wore some version of sweatpants in dark green or navy blue or bright red, with white or maroon or black sweatshirts, and turtlenecks underneath. On a whim, they'd decided to wear mismatched socks—polka dots with stripes, pink with purple, plaid with checks—and were having fun showing off their choices.

Selena came to stand beside Chris. "You found different clothes? Whose are they?"

"One of the maintenance staff, I guess." He hitched up the black jeans, which kept sliding down on his hips. "He's about my height, but maybe thirty pounds heavier." The Hawkridge sweatshirt—burgundy with a gold hawk emblem over the heart—hung in extra folds around his waist.

She thought for a minute. "That's probably Mr. Trevino. He's nice."

"That's good." Chris winked at her. "I'd hate to be wearing a bad guy's jeans and sweatshirt." The girls had an apparently endless supply of clothes, and even Jayne had managed to change pants and shirts most days, but the wardrobe he'd arrived in had gotten too dirty to wear.

Yet another sign that this adventure would be coming to an end. Chris didn't relish the prospect.

The case clock on the wall beside the front doors chimed five and, at that exact moment, Jayne stepped into the entry hall.

Her eyes widened as she took in their appearance. "You all look wonderful. So festive." She glanced at the girls' feet and smiled. "I love the socks."

But Chris, along with the girls, kept silent, stunned by the change they saw in Tommy herself. The clothes were more or less the same, dark pants and sweater, white sneakers. She'd put on a green turtleneck in place of the standard white one. The indirect glow of their flashlights showed off the creaminess of her skin in contrast to the bright color.

The most startling difference, though, was with her hair. For once the severe ponytail was gone. The mahogany waves floated softly around her face, then fell into glossy curves at her shoulders.

She looks, Chris thought, *about ten years younger. They probably never realized that she's not old, or even middle-aged. She's still young, and should be living that way.*

"Wow, Ms. Thomas." Beth voiced the words they all were thinking. "You look beautiful!"

"Thank you." She bowed her head. "Then we all look beautiful together." She cocked her head as she looked Chris up and down. "Even Mr. Hammond, in his borrowed threads."

"Are we ready?" Haley had appointed herself the leader of the procession and the other girls had let her have her way. "Line up, everybody."

"That means two by two," Chris told Jayne as the students got into place. "You're beside me at the end."

She stepped into the designated spot, but didn't look at him, or smile or say a word.

"We have decided to call this our Peace Day," Haley announced. "We want to celebrate peace as it exists and create even more peace. Our Peace Day carol is 'Dona Nobis Pacem.' Everyone should sing along."

Chris frowned, trying to translate the Latin.

"'Give Us Peace,'" Jayne said quietly, just as the girls began to sing.

The quiet words were amplified by the acoustics of the big, two-story entry hall. When the music broke into two parts, and then three, the harmonies echoed all around.

"This is what heaven sounds like," Chris murmured, to himself as much as Jayne.

"This is why I'm here," she answered, nodding.

Yolanda and Sarah opened the double doors and Haley led the way into the hall. They all filed into the kitchen and took their places at the table, still singing, with Chris and Jayne entering last.

As the final notes floated away into silence, Jayne clasped her hands under her chin and gazed at the second surprise of the evening. "Oh, my."

All the flashlights had been set around the perimeter of the kitchen, while the table had been set with candles to light the meal. Around the base of each candle was an arrangement of greenery—pine, mistletoe and cedar sprigs with holly leaves and bright red berries. A sheet of aluminum foil underneath the greens reflected the flickering lights.

"This is beautiful," she told them. "And so creative. Who needs electricity when we have such elegant and resourceful light?" Then she sniffed the air. "And the food smells fantastic. Let's eat."

The food was more delicious than any dinner Chris could remember. Jayne sat beside him, contentment radiating around her like a candle's glow. The girls still acted like teenagers—there was a certain amount of playing with food and giggling, along with some arguing over who got to pull the wishbones on the birds. They were kids, after all. Kids who loved each other. Kids who were all part of the same family.

He wondered if Jayne wanted children of her own. Working with teenagers all day and then coming home to a baby might be more than she wanted to take on. Especially if her husband wasn't home every night.

Maybe her husband would have to think about changing jobs.

After the elaborate meal, cleaning up the kitchen took longer than usual, but the girls pitched in with an amazing lack of complaints.

Then Haley resumed her mistress of ceremonies role. "The Peace Tree awaits," she said. "Follow me."

A few snorts greeted her dramatic tone. Hurt flared in her face and for a second Chris thought hostilities would break out.

But Jayne stepped up beside her. "Could you sing one more round of 'Dona Nobis Pacem' as we go in? That was so beautiful."

As Jayne no doubt knew, no one could carry on a disagreement while singing "Give Us Peace." The girls fell into their double line again as they crossed the hall into the library.

Chris hadn't seen the finished project before he went upstairs to change his clothes, so the overall effect surprised him. Jayne stopped still in the doorway and he stood just behind her, taking in the scene as the girls wandered the room admiring their handiwork.

The garlands of pine branches he'd helped wire together were draped across the tall windows, silhouetted against the silvery light outside. Holly twigs with their berries had been tucked into nooks and crannies all over the room, between books, at the corners of paintings and maps, into vases and decorative pottery. Set on every available table were stainless steel bowls of all sizes—no doubt borrowed from the main kitchen—filled with glittery pinecones and balls of crushed aluminum foil and more holly.

In the center of this splendor stood the Peace Tree. The slender evergreen they'd brought back from the woods had been transformed. Aluminum foil icicles hung from the branches to twinkle in the firelight. Sprays of holly provided touches of red, with more glittery pinecones adding sparkle. The top of the tree held a bird figure fashioned out of foil— a dove in flight, Chris realized, with holly in its mouth instead of an olive branch. A seasonal symbol of peace.

"Terrific," Chris said, when he'd taken in every detail. "You girls are geniuses. I'm only sorry there aren't more people able to share your vision and your celebration tonight."

Jayne, still standing motionless in front of him, hadn't said a word.

"I think Ms. Thomas is stunned speechless," he joked. "Did you ever believe you'd see your headmistress without a word to say?" The silence was stretching beyond bearable, and the girls' faces were beginning to reflect their concerns that something was wrong. He gave Jayne's shoulder a little nudge.

She jumped, and seemed to wake up. "I'm sorry, I'm just so surprised and amazed and delighted, I was in a trance for a moment there." Moving into the room, she gave each girl a tight hug. "You all have created something truly beautiful, a celebration coming out of the care you have for each other and, I think, your hopes for the world in which you'll make your futures. I am immensely proud of all of you. Happy Day of Peace!"

They all returned the salute. "Happy Day of Peace."

After some time spent talking by the fire, as well as seconds on trifle for everyone, the usual evening rituals resumed. The girls tucked themselves into their bedding and turned their flashlights off so that only the fire lit the room. After such a busy day, Chris figured they'd fall asleep early. Then one more day to play in the snow before—

"Okay, Mr. Hammond, tonight's the night." Selena and Beth were sitting up, staring at him. Yolanda had propped herself on one elbow. Taryn, Haley, Sarah and Monique were obviously quite awake.

"Tonight's the night for...?" He let the phrase trail off, hoping for any answer but the one they gave.

Monique rolled her eyes. "Don't play dumb. You got us hooked, telling us about a guy who killed the girl he loved. So tonight's the night we get to find out what happened. And why."

"We've been waiting," Sarah pointed out.

Selena nodded. "You owe us."

Chris winced and shook his head. "It's late. You're tired. I'm tired."

"Too bad," Beth said.

"We might not even be here tomorrow night," Haley added. "We heard those men who came this morning. If the road gets plowed tomorrow, they'll probably send trucks up here to take us back where there's electricity and phones and heat and stuff."

"Then we'd never know the end." Taryn sounded pitiful.

"You can't avoid us by fixing the fire."

Yolanda had guessed exactly what he was doing. He'd gotten up to put on a couple of logs and then stood poking at them, with his back to the girls, trying to invent an excuse.

Because he no longer had any desire to reveal what had happened that Christmas Eve twelve years ago. Partly because the events of that night reflected badly on who he had been and what he'd done. And partly because he didn't want to share with these recovering girls the harsh truths behind those events.

Mostly, though, because he didn't want to tell Jayne the rest of the story. Not in front of her students. Not until he had a chance to tell her other things that mattered more, now, than the past.

She had taken up her usual seat in the corner of the couch. He looked at her as he sought to escape the trap he'd set up for himself.

Jayne met his eyes, her own fierce but determined. "I think you should finish the story. We all want to know how it ends."

Chris pulled in a deep breath and blew it out hard.

"Okay." Taking a chair, he braced his hands on his knees.

"After that night on the mountain, Chase and Juliet grew closer every time they saw each other. The next Christmas, he gave her a necklace with an oval of polished granite made from a stone he'd picked up that night at Little Bear. Juliet never took the necklace off.

"For two years she continued to visit in the summers and winters. They spent as much time alone together as they could, and, uh, fooled around. A lot."

"'Fooled around?' What's that mean?"

Taryn looked at Monique. "They're making out. Sucking face. Tonsil hockey. Got it?"

"Well, how'm I supposed to know old-fashioned words like 'fooled around'?"

"Anyway," Chris said loudly, to prevent an argument, "the summer Juliet turned seventeen, they made love for the first time."

Taryn looked at Monique. "Do you need a translation?"

"No."

* * *

With a year left of high school, they couldn't be together all the time, but they talked about going to the same college, getting married and having a life together with adventures all over the world. The train ride between Philadelphia and New York was only a couple of hours, and Chase started spending weekends in the city, sleeping in a hostel and seeing Juliet whenever she could get away from the house.

The phone calls to Philly and the weekend absences alerted Juliet's parents to what was going on. Chase's parents got involved, too, and there was talk about private boarding schools and comments like, "too young to be in love" and "if it's real, a little separation won't change anything." Chase and Juliet didn't believe that any more than any other teenage couple ever did. They kept trying to be together, but their parents cut back on allowances and credit cards, which made things tough.

Toughest of all was Christmas, when Juliet's parents refused to let her visit her grandmother. She threatened a hunger strike and retreated to her room, but they kept their word. Chase went to Charlie's house and moped around for three weeks before going back to Philadelphia. As soon as he could, he tried calling Juliet.

Her number had been changed—something her parents had done to them several times before. Juliet had always called within hours to give him the new number. Chase waited three weeks, but she didn't call.

So he cut class and went to her school in New York to find her, only to be told by her friends that Juliet had been transferred to a private school. They didn't know the name, they didn't know her new phone number and they weren't sure they could get her a message, but they'd try.

* * *

"What is this, like, the Dark Ages?" Monique punched her pillow. "How can they treat kids like that?"

"I'd have run away," Beth said. "They'd never have found me."

Chris managed half a grin. "Chase did cut loose from his family, as soon as he graduated from high school. He went to live with Charlie and got himself a job in town—in the same general store he'd caught Juliet stealing from. He figured that when she could get free, she would find him there, where they belonged."

"Did she come to him?" Jayne asked the question, and they all turned to look at her. "Did she escape New York?"

"The next Christmas," Chris told her, "Juliet arrived at her grandmother's house. She called Charlie, and Chase was there within the hour."

A huge sigh blew through the library as all the girls relaxed.

"What took her so long?" Taryn asked.

"The school they moved Juliet to used drugs to keep her under control," Chris said. "In a way it does sound like the Dark Ages. She stopped taking the pills, got her brain back and at the first opportunity just walked away with nothing but the clothes she wore."

Juliet's parents wanted her back, of course. She would inherit a fortune from her grandmother, and more from her parents, so they wanted to control who she would marry, where she lived and what she did. Chase's parents had cut off his inheritance, so now he was just a grocery boy trying to marry a rich girl, and that made him completely unacceptable.

"He didn't care about the money. Chase wanted to get married and start their life of adventure together. But…"

Chris paused a moment, hesitating over the rest.

"What do you mean, 'but?'" Selena demanded. "How could there be a 'but' at this point?"

Nothing to do but go on. "Juliet avoided the idea of getting married," Chris explained. "She'd been so eager before, but now Chase would ask, and she would say, 'Yes, yes, someday soon.' But he couldn't get her to commit to a definite day."

She was different in other ways, as well. She was skittish about kisses, about making love. Only if they'd had some wine, or beer, and she was a little drunk—or more than a little—did she relax and become the lover he remembered.

Chris halted when Jayne got up from the sofa. He thought she might be leaving the library, but instead she walked to one of the French doors and stood staring into the snowy garden. She had braced herself, he thought, with her arms crossed over her breasts and her hands close to her face.

He didn't know how to make what was coming any easier for her.

Christmas Eve, Juliet's grandmother asked Charlie and Chase to join them for dinner. They had a nice meal and, since it was snowing, Charlie accepted an invitation to spend the night.

Once the grandparents went to bed, Chase sat with Juliet in front of the fire. He put his arms around her, tried to kiss her, but Juliet pulled away.

At this point, Chase—a frustrated teenage male—lost his

temper. "What's the matter with you? You don't want me to touch you anymore. Maybe that's why I couldn't find you, couldn't get in contact with you. Is there somebody else?"

"Don't be stupid." She was looking out the window at the snow. "There won't ever be anyone else."

So Chase went to join her at the window. "Then love me," he said, not being very bright. He put his arms around Juliet and pulled her into a kiss.

After enduring a moment or two, she exploded out of his hold. "Don't," she pleaded, hiding her face in her hands. "Please don't make me."

The words, the way she said them, helped Chase grow up between one minute and the next. He recognized real trouble behind Juliet's actions, and knew he would have to discover the source.

So he said, "Let's go for a drive."

They'd done this several times in the past, taken her grandmother's old convertible out for an evening on the mountain roads...but never in the winter and never in the snow. Still, the suggestion brought a smile to Juliet's face and that was all that mattered to Chase.

They bundled up in their coats and hats and gloves, lowered the convertible's roof and sailed down the long driveway. He drove a reasonable speed and he kept his eyes on the road. Juliet stuck to her side of the bench seat, and Chase didn't even try to hold her hand. He hoped that would make it easier for her to talk to him.

So they rode on through the snowy night and, eventually, Juliet revealed what had happened to her. Last Christmas, in New York, her parents had introduced her to the man they wanted her to marry. He was old, in his thirties. He would take good care of her, they said. All she had to do was be nice to him, let him have his way.

They threw an engagement party, with a Christmas tree in every room. Juliet had been locked in her bedroom until they came to get her to introduce the "happy couple." But when the door opened, it wasn't her mother or her father. Her fiancé came in…and he locked the door behind him.

Chris stopped to take several breaths. His heart hammered against his ribs. His hands had clenched into fists and he had to think about relaxing his fingers. Then he continued.

The man raped Juliet. When he finished, he told her parents he would not marry her because she wasn't a virgin.

When he paused again, the girls didn't say anything. He shouldn't have burdened these young women with the grim truth. But he couldn't stop now.

Chase had pulled off the road—he was too upset to drive. He wanted to kill Juliet's parents, and the man who had forced her. He hated himself for not being there, for not keeping her safe. And he hated himself for wanting her when she'd been treated so cruelly.

So he started driving again, and this time he wasn't careful to stay slow and safe. The snow blew like sand across the pavement as they fishtailed around the curves, coasting down the hills and charging up the inclines. Snowflakes stung their cheeks and burned their eyes, and the speedometer crept higher. Juliet didn't ask him to stop. She laughed and shrieked and urged him on.

Until, of course, he made a mistake. Chase rounded a blind corner in the other lane and looked up into the headlights of an oncoming car. He braked, slid and jerked the wheel. The convertible bucked and went onto the shoulder of the road, through the guardrail and straight down the side of the mountain.

Chapter Twelve

"Chase woke up in the hospital a week later. He had been thrown clear of the convertible, which burst into flames. Juliet's body had burned to ash in the car."

Chris stirred in his chair and cleared his throat. "So there you go. That's how he killed the girl he loved. Not a very cheerful story for Peace Day. But you asked for the end."

Around him, the girls had all dissolved into tears at some point during the story. Now, as the tears dried, the questions and comments started.

"Did she come back to haunt him?"

"I hope he went to New York and got even with her parents and the rapist."

"Maybe we could have a séance and contact her spirit."

"Why weren't they wearing their seat belts?"

"Then they both would've burned up. That'd be worse."

"I wonder if he ever found another girlfriend."

They looked to him for answers, but Chris just shrugged his shoulders. The girls talked quietly about the story for a while, but sleep captured all of them soon enough.

Only then did he look over at Jayne. She hadn't moved, hadn't even breathed, so far as he could tell, since the last time he'd glanced her way. He stood up from his chair and took a step in her direction.

She put up a hand, signaling for him to stop, and came to him instead. He tried to read her face, but she was keeping every emotion locked away.

"I need some time," she said in a low voice. "Don't follow me."

Her footsteps sounded in the hall. Chris heard a door brush across the floor, and the click as it closed again, with Jayne on the other side.

Now she knew everything. Did she believe him?

Did she remember?

IN THE STOREROOM, Jayne pulled on her coat and boots. Then she went outside.

With the full moon like a lantern overhead, she followed the girls' tracks through the snow around to the front of the manor. Past the front steps, lines of footsteps squiggled in all directions across the lawn, like a bizarre map carved into white stone. She smiled, thinking of the games she'd watched the girls play out here, chasing each other and floundering though the snow. A host of angels lay off to one side. Three snow folks stood sentry on the other.

She reached a point where the students had all turned back. One set of prints continued forward, however, and those she followed, stepping where Chris had stepped because it made the walking easier. Although he'd wandered a bit, looking at the cottages for guests and teachers, Jayne had no doubt about his final destination. Big boot prints on her lavender front porch confirmed her assumption. Chris had been inside her house.

Leaving her boots outside, as he probably had, Jayne walked through the rooms she'd lived in for almost three years now. With windows on all sides, the house was never completely dark unless she drew the drapes, and tonight the snow reflected bright moonlight through every pane. She didn't expect to see any damage, or find anything taken, didn't have many possessions beyond her books that someone else would want. A teacher's life rarely offered luxury, and that's all she'd lived.

At least, all she remembered living.

In the bedroom, she knelt by the bed and pulled a plastic storage box out from underneath the four-poster. The plastic was stiff with cold, so it took a minute to work the top off.

Inside were papers relating to her grandmother's death, the sale of her house and land, the small insurance policy she'd left and the few investments she'd owned. One file folder contained photographs Elizabeth Jayne Thomas had kept on her wall. A yellowed snapshot showed a smiling family of four—dad, mom, daughter, son—posed on the porch of a suburban home. Mother and daughter shared the same reddish-brown curls and hazel eyes as had Elizabeth Jayne before her hair went completely white. Dad and son had been sandy-haired, with dark brown eyes.

This was the family Jayne had grown up knowing, had mourned and longed for. She'd cried with her grandmother on the anniversaries of their deaths. There was a wedding shot of the parents, baby photos of the son and daughter. All babies look pretty much the same.

Jayne set the pictures aside and lifted out a small cedar chest, the kind popular in gift shops throughout the Smoky Mountains. This one had rested on Elizabeth Jayne's dresser, never opened in Jayne's presence. She'd gone through the trinkets after her grandmother's death and found nothing of real value, nothing she wanted to wear in remembrance. But she hadn't been ready to throw out her grandmother's treasures, either. So she'd tucked the box away.

Now she fingered past the gold-filled chains, the ceramic flower pins and faux pearl earrings, the crystal bead bracelets. The object of her search lay at the bottom, in a corner, hidden by shadows and the absence of lamplight. But Jayne found it by touch—cold, smooth, flat—and pulled it out.

This pendant had puzzled her because of its uniqueness. An oval piece of polished granite had little in common with the rest of Elizabeth Jayne's jewelry. And now she knew why.

Chris had given this pendant, on its chain, to Juliet. Elizabeth Jayne had hidden the pendant and called the girl who wore it Jayne. Jayne Thomas.

"Are you all right?" The glare of a flashlight filled the room.

She shrieked and dropped the stone. "What are you doing here?" Scrambling to her feet, she stared at the man standing in the doorway to her bedroom. "I told you not to follow me."

"When I realized you'd gone outside, I got worried."

"You've left the girls alone, exactly what I didn't want to happen." She'd lost control of her voice, which sounded high and squeaky.

"Settle down. I woke Sarah and she said she'd keep watch while we were gone."

With her eyes squeezed shut, Jayne struggled to regain some sense of balance and self-possession. "You don't have the right to walk into my house uninvited." Then she laughed. "Of course, that didn't stop you the first time."

"I'm trying to help you, Jayne."

She opened her eyes to glare at him. "Why keep up the pretense? You've been waiting for this moment all week, haven't you? Call me by the right name—call me Juliet."

Taking a step toward her, he said, "You remember?"

"No. I don't remember any more than I ever did. But here's your proof." She bent to pick up the pendant and held it out in the palm of her shaking hand. "It's what you wanted. Proof."

He kept his hands in his coat pockets. "Yes, I'd say that is the stone I gave Juliet. She never took it off. What do you think happened?"

"I don't know. I can't remember." Pushing past him, she hurried through the house. She would have rushed out into the snow but she had to stop and put her boots on. So of course Chris caught up with her before she'd finished. And since he hadn't bothered to take his boots off, he walked beside her when she stepped off the porch.

"But what do you *think* happened?" he asked again.

The cold air and clear sky poured a bit of calm into her mind. "I can only guess. Maybe she…I…wandered away into the woods. Elizabeth Jayne found me, realized I didn't remember anything and…and adopted me."

"You said you woke up from a coma."

"That's what she told me." She stopped without warning, letting him walk on, getting some distance between them. "Don't you see, all I know is what she told me?"

He turned back, and they stared at each other in the moonlight. Finally, Chris took a deep breath. "It's hard to accept that Juliet could be alive and not know me. Not remember *us*. I've lost the best part of my past."

"It's hard to understand how someone could pretend to love and care for me and be lying to me with every word." She opened her hands in a helpless gesture, then let them fall to her sides. "I've lost the only past I knew."

She started walking again, and they continued back to the

manor together. "The girls do not need to know about this," she warned as they passed the walls of Emmeline's garden. "You've told them too much as it is."

They reached the side door, and she paused to look at him before going in. She couldn't read his face, couldn't tell what he was thinking.

"I will continue to use Jayne Thomas as my name, whatever the facts might be."

He tilted his head. "I didn't expect anything else."

His simple comment told her the final truth—Chris wanted Juliet, not Jayne. Even if his Juliet no longer existed.

"Well, then we've reached the end of the story, haven't we? The mystery is solved, the pieces put together and everybody's satisfied." Swallowing tears, Jayne pushed open the door and entered the hallway.

"Not by a long shot," Chris muttered, following.

AFTER TENDING THE FIRE, Chris went back to the infirmary to sleep that night. Being stretched out on a hard bed was more restful than trying to sleep curled up in an armchair.

Besides, he had thinking to do, thinking that wouldn't be encouraged by having Jayne just across the room. She'd taken a real blow tonight. Finding out she'd been raped, and hearing the account of their crash down the mountain, would have been enough of a shock, without discovering the lies her "grandmother" had given her as memories.

He wanted to talk about all of this with Jayne, wanted to hold her while she sorted through the lies and the truths of the last twelve years. Together they could reconstruct the past, and then leave it behind as they went ahead with the rest of their lives. Together.

As soon as he'd seen her, on her knees in the bedroom of

the lavender cottage, he'd recognized the barriers she'd erected between them, like a snow fort with walls a foot thick. He'd need a battering ram to break through.

Unfortunately, he'd already done all the battering his conscience would allow. He'd been so stupidly sure of himself, busting in and planning to force Jayne Thomas to admit her true identity. All he'd thought about was what *he* deserved, regardless of the cost to Jayne.

So now he had the truth, and he *deserved* every bit of it. Juliet hadn't died that night. She was alive and well and living in Ridgeville. And she didn't remember him at all. How about that for a twist of fate?

With the skimpy pillow twisted under his head and the blankets twisted around his body, Chris finally fell into an uneasy sleep. In general, he rarely remembered his dreams, but on this night he revisited the accident over and over again, each time waking up as he was tossed out of the car. He came to rest in different places—against a tree, in a deep, violent river, on the rocks of the mountainside. And every time Juliet glided past him, just out of reach. Finally, as the first light of dawn outlined the treetops with silver, Chris fell into a deep, peaceful sleep.

Only seconds later, or so it seemed, he sat straight up in bed, awakened by the loud, angry ring of a telephone.

THE SHRILL NOISE, after days of silence and a night without sleep, didn't make sense at first. After three rings, Jayne remembered how to answer the phone.

When she said goodbye and hung up, she turned to find seven expectant faces gathered around her.

Sarah spoke for them all. "The phone works?"

Jayne nodded. "That was Deputy Greeley. The snowplow

will be here by noon, and the drive should be clear before dark." She took a deep breath. "We can load into one of the vans and drive down to Ridgeville in time for dinner."

The festival of rejoicing lasted through breakfast and kitchen cleanup.

"Our last day of oatmeal," Monique crowed. "Tomorrow morning, it's bacon and eggs with all the trimmings."

"I'm taking a two-hour bath." Beth closed her eyes in contemplation. "With bubbles up to my nose."

"Not if I get to the tub first," Selena teased.

"I'll throw you for it." Beth held up a hand. "One, two, three." A fast game of Rock, Paper, Scissors left Beth the undisputed title of First Bather.

"Can we call home?" Sarah asked. "I think my parents are worried."

"Everyone can make a ten-minute call this morning," Jayne told them. "We'll go in reverse alphabetical order."

Yolanda smiled on her way to the phone. "Thanks."

Jayne was at the kitchen table with her third cup of coffee, still timing phone calls, when Chris came in.

"We're reunited with civilization, I gather." His voice sounded even rougher than usual. When he sat down facing her, he looked tired. "Is there more good news?"

She told him the arrangements for the day. "You can take one of the school cars and go to your grandfather's house. I know you must be worried about him."

Chris acknowledged the point with a shrug. "I'll be glad to see him." He took a long swig of coffee. "Where will you and the girls stay?"

"Good question. I'll call the hotel when the phone is free to see if they have enough rooms for tonight. Or to make a dinner reservation, at least." She smiled, hoping to spark an answering grin from him. "Nobody is cooking this evening, if I can help it."

His mouth twitched, then curved slightly. "I'm thinking about a medium-rare steak, myself. Nothing that resembles a stew."

"Or soup."

"Or a sandwich of any kind." His eyes had brightened, and Jayne felt some of the life come back into her own spirit.

"I guess you're still responsible for these hellions," he said, nodding at Taryn on the phone with her grandfather. Holding the receiver to her ear, the girl heard Chris's comment and stuck her tongue out at him.

"Unless all their families show up to take them away tonight." The thought depressed her. "We've still got two weeks of vacation left before classes start again. Some of them might go home, but I suspect several will stay."

Chris set his mug down with a clank. "Will there ever come a time when you aren't in charge? When you only have to consider yourself?"

She didn't know where his anger came from, but her temper sparked in response. "What else do I have? Where else would I go?"

At that moment, Taryn hung up the phone and turned around. "What do we do now?"

Jayne got stiffly to her feet. "I think we have some house-keeping to take care of."

She spent the morning in the dormitory with the girls, requiring them to collect their dirty clothes in piles and clean up their rooms, even to the extent of sweeping the floor.

"We're not going to be here," Haley muttered, trying to use the broom with one hand. "What difference does it make if our room is neat?"

"It'll be nicer to come back to." Monique took the broom

out of the younger girl's hand. "Let me do this. You're just making a mess."

Once their rooms were neat, Jayne had them each pack a bag for three nights. "If we need to be gone longer, we'll come back for more clothes. Or maybe," she said, eyeing Selena's mountain of laundry, "we'll spend a day at the Wash-A-Rama."

With their bags lined up in the entry hall, they returned to the kitchen in time to see the snowplow erupt onto the circular front drive. Jayne allowed the girls to go watch, with the admonition to be careful and stay out of the way.

She put on her coat and went to supervise, of course. The steps and walks Chris had cleared meant she didn't have to wear boots or tramp through the snow. But she couldn't say thank-you because he'd stayed out of sight all morning.

After one more soup-and-sandwich lunch, the afternoon proved to be perhaps the most difficult four hours of the whole ordeal. Seven girls wanted to be somewhere else, a somewhere that included all the conveniences modern life had to offer. Sitting by the fire had lost its charm. They didn't want to read, play games or work puzzles. Even their beautiful Peace Tree couldn't hold their attention.

"I want music," Selena said. "I want to dance!" Singing to herself, she gyrated around the library in a very energetic version of salsa dancing.

Taryn stood at the window, watching the melting snow drip off nearby branches. "I'm bringing my favorite movies with me." She listed all the latest fantasy epics. "That'll keep me going for at least three days."

"Hotel rooms don't have DVDs," Haley said in a disparaging tone. "You only get to watch what's on their menu."

"Well, then, I'll go buy a DVD and hook it up."

Beth rolled her eyes. "Yeah, right. I'm sure you know how to hook up a DVD player."

"I do," Taryn insisted. "I'm not stupid, like some people."

Beth got to her feet. "Like who?"

Jayne stepped up beside them. "Each of you, take a separate corner of this room and stay there. We're not having this kind of argument. Not today. Not any day."

The two disengaged and went to different parts of the library. Jayne eyed the other girls sitting around waiting. "Everyone understands the plan, I hope. A peaceful afternoon until we are ready to leave?"

The five girls nodded and returned to being bored and sleepy. Sarah, at least, had a book to read. Monique fidgeted; Yolanda snored lightly as she napped. Selena painted her fingernails, and then Haley's.

One of the outside doors banged open, and they all jumped.

"You know it's Mr. Hammond," Selena said, giggling. "He's always doing that."

"You're right." Chris stood in the door to the library. In his arms he carried a huge stainless steel bowl, with another of equal size turned upside down as a top. "Quick, somebody go get bowls and spoons. I have something special here."

He went to the library table farthest from the fireplace. Looking at the mahogany tabletop, he quirked an eyebrow. "Maybe we need a plastic cloth, too. Or plastic sacks. Something waterproof."

Jayne lifted an eyebrow as she looked at him. "What have you done?"

"Quick," he said. "I'm freezing to death."

Yolanda brought bowls and spoons and Jayne laid out the plastic tablecloth they'd been using in the kitchen. With a sigh, Chris set his burden on the table.

"This, ladies, is a delicacy only available in winter, and only when it snows. Not only that, but you must have the purest, cleanest snow for this particular treat."

Haley gazed up at him as if he were a magician. "What is it?"

Edging the tips of his fingers under the rim of the top bowl, Chris revealed his treasure with a flourish. "Snow cream!"

When they all just stared at him, he took a step back. "You don't know what snow cream is? How sad is that? Look."

From his coat pocket, he drew a bottle of pure maple syrup, no doubt from the main kitchen. "I hiked way up the mountain to find this snow—no footprints or paw prints or hoofprints anywhere near, just rock underneath and rocks above. Now we'll take this pure snow and drizzle it with syrup, like so."

He poured a thin stream of maple syrup over the snow in the bowl.

"Like a golden cobweb," Sarah said.

He nodded. "And then…we eat."

Jayne wondered, as she savored her own snow cream, how many times this week she had stood back and watched Chris Hammond make some kind of magic for these girls. Not with disappearing bunnies or cascading card tricks, but with his own generous spirit and cheerful good nature. A situation that might very well have aggravated them all had been enjoyable, most of the time, because he'd been there.

Her girls would miss him. The rest of their vacation simply would not be the same. Warmer, perhaps, and more comfortable. But not nearly as much fun.

And Jayne didn't have to remember a single moment before this past week to know she would miss Chris Hammond for the rest of her life.

JAYNE DROVE the largest school van to the circular drive in front of the manor and parked by the steps. The girls carried their bags out from the entry hall for Chris to load into the luggage space.

Each girl gave him a hug after he'd taken her bag. He stopped trying to remember all the different ways they said thank-you—he was too busy keeping his tears contained.

A small sedan parked behind the van, and Jayne got out. She handed Chris the keys. "Feel free to keep this car as long as you're in town. When you're finished, just leave it with the sheriff's department. They'll get it back to the school."

He nodded. "Do I have to fill the tank up before I turn it in?"

She gave a rueful smile. "Consider the gas your Peace Holiday gift."

"I don't have one for you."

The girls were playing around in the relatively warm afternoon, checking out the melting snow, rediscovering plants and rocks and benches that had been hidden by the blizzard. Jayne looked at them all, and then shook her head. "You've given us a week of gifts, from the fire that kept us warm to the games you played and…" her eyes met his "…and the stories you told. None of us will forget."

"Promise?"

"Amnesia jokes are not funny." She frowned at him and then, suddenly, put her arms around his neck and her lips to his cheek.

"Thank you," Jayne whispered. "You'll never know…."

Her words trailed off, and her arms closed tightly around his neck. Then she stepped back, making no effort to hold back the tears.

"Take care. Drive carefully," she added, with emphasis. "No more accidents."

He held up his hand. "I swear."

Turning away, she called to the girls. "Everybody in the van. Make sure you have your purse, bag, book, whatever you brought out here. No arguing," she said, even as someone inside the van protested, "about who sits where. Let's just get to town."

With the driver's door open, she looked at Chris again. "I've checked the building and locked the doors. All you have to do is drive away." For a moment she looked down, as if she wanted to say something else.

But she simply waved, got into the van and started the engine. As they followed the circular drive, the girls rolled down the windows and put their arms out to wave goodbye, reminding Chris of a beetle with legs too short to reach the ground.

The van disappeared into the forest lining the long drive from the highway to Hawkridge Manor, the drive he'd walked a week ago with anger and determination overcoming the pain of his injuries.

Well, he wasn't angry anymore. But there was plenty of pain left to go around. Some of that pain would simply have to fade with time. Nothing else could be done. But he had caused some of it, and he intended to make amends.

Starting with his plans for dinner tonight.

Chapter Thirteen

The romantic, candlelit meal Chris had started planning for that evening failed to materialize.

He arrived at Charlie's cabin to find a note on the door: "Dr Appt." The doctor's office had sent him to the hospital. At his granddad's weekly chemotherapy session, the doctor had detected a problem with Charlie's heartbeat.

So instead of getting cleaned up and buying flowers, Chris spent the late afternoon and evening hours sitting by his grandfather's bed, holding the old man's thin, dry hand.

"What am I doing here, anyway, wearing this stupid excuse for a nightgown and hooked up to all these machines?" Charlie rolled his head fretfully on the pillow. "Why such a fuss? We all know I'm headed for the exit door, one way or the other."

"The rest of us would like to delay that exit as long as possible. More water?" Chris picked up the pitcher to fill the glass on the bed tray, then realized Charlie hadn't taken a sip since the last time he'd filled it.

"Hell, no, I don't want water." His granddad pushed the rolling tray away. "I want to know what you're doing here with me in the first place. You look like death warmed over."

Chris winced, and Charlie cackled. "Well, you do. When's the last time you had a shave, boy?"

"The morning I left your house."

"And you haven't changed your clothes in about as long."

"Pretty much."

"No wonder you stink."

"I do?" He sniffed a fold of his shirt. "I guess I do."

"But you say you found Juliet?" Charlie shook his head. "It's hard to believe. I mean, what else were we supposed to think? When I got there, you were lying up against a tree, dead for all I knew, with that car burning like an inferno nearby. Nobody thought she could have just walked away."

Chris rubbed his eyes with his free hand. "We'll probably never know exactly what happened, or how she ended up with Elizabeth Jayne Thomas. Unless Jayne remembers."

Charlie didn't answer; he'd dozed off again. He'd been doing that since Chris arrived—falling asleep, then popping awake again to resume the conversation exactly where they'd left off. The nurse said the medications were to blame.

For the first time in five hours, Chris released Charlie's hand and slumped into his chair, head back and eyes closed. He'd been looking forward to that change of clothes, the shower and shave Charlie said he needed. By now he should have been sharing a gourmet dinner with Jayne, making her smile, undoing some of the damage from the last few days. Even with seven girls watching, he'd have managed to at least hold her hand.

"But you say she doesn't remember a thing," Charlie continued, as if his fifteen-minute nap had never happened. "Not any of the time you two spent together, or how she ended up with this other grandmother?"

Chris lifted his head and opened his eyes. "Not a minute."

"Maybe that's all to the good. Some of what happened, she shouldn't have to live with."

"Right." He hated to be the one who'd brought the rape back to her. And he didn't know how to take it away again. Those scary dreams of hers were as close as she ever needed to come to remembering.

Charlie tapped his fingers on the bed. "In the meantime, you've got some work to do."

"I think so."

"Sounds to me like she's got good reason not to trust you."

"Yes."

His granddad scowled at him. "So what are you doing hanging around here?"

"I came to spend time with you, Charlie."

"Well, six hours is about as much time as we ever spent in the same room together, son. I'm getting tired of waking up and seeing you staring at me."

"So you're telling me to leave?"

"I'm telling you to go get some rest. And then see about wooing this woman you want. Bring her to me—I'll set her straight."

Grinning, Chris got to his feet. "Is that a threat?"

"You bet. Now go." Charlie waved him out of the room. "I'll still be around tomorrow."

"I'm holding you to that."

After so many hours in a heated building, Chris was relieved to step outside into the cold night air. The world of electricity seemed strange after a week without. He'd lost his tolerance for asphalt parking lots under the glare of bright white lights and the intrusion of illuminated building signs. The stars didn't shine so brightly with all this competition. He really missed the blackness of the Hawkridge nights.

Driving down Ridgeville's Main Street, he was surprised to see all the lighted Christmas decorations—shining Santas, wreaths and bells and snowmen. A lighted Christmas tree stood in practically every window. After the girls' Peace Day celebration, Chris had practically forgotten about Christmas.

Then, as he registered at the reception desk of the Ridgeville Inn, he realized today was Christmas Day. His weary eyes finally saw the garlands of greenery hung from the doors and windows and the staircase banister. He turned toward the elevator and, amazed, took a step backward at the sight of a huge Christmas tree decorated with gold and maroon glass balls and thousands of twinkling lights. Somewhere—the dining room, maybe—a piano played Christmas music.

He should have wished Charlie a Merry Christmas before he left the hospital; they might not share another one. Regret made Chris even wearier.

Once he got to his room, a long, hot shower revived his spirits somewhat. Shaving, he decided, could wait until tomorrow. Clean underwear, socks, sweatpants and a T-shirt definitely made the world a better place. The mirror in the bathroom showed that his bruises had turned an ugly shade of green, splotched with yellow and brown.

Those old aches and pains, he thought, were probably not as much punishment as he deserved.

Taking a candy bar and a soda from the room's minibar, Chris sat on the bed, staring at the phone. What was Jayne doing with her Christmas night? Not celebrating, he knew. What would she say if he wished her a Merry Christmas?

Would she talk to him at all?

The phone stared back without answering. There was only one way to find out.

JAYNE'S EVENING HADN'T turned out as she'd expected.

On the drive from the school into Ridgeville, the girls had concluded that their choice for dinner would be pizza.

Sarah, riding in the front passenger seat, looked over at Jayne. "Is that okay, Ms. Thomas?"

"I think it sounds delicious. And we won't have to dress up." Since all Jayne really wanted to do was crawl into bed and pull the covers over her head, a slight delay for pizza didn't matter very much.

As they reached the outskirts of town, the girls began to exclaim at the holiday decorations on houses, barns and fences. When they turned onto Main Street, the shops were closed but the windows displayed every sort of holiday scene.

Jayne glanced at the date on the dashboard clock display. "Good grief. It's Christmas Day."

Sarah laughed. "That's right, it is. Merry Christmas, everybody." A chorus of greetings responded.

"Happy Yule."

"Mazel tov."

"Merry Merry!"

"Here's to world peace," Yolanda said. And all the girls laughed.

Jayne wondered what Chris and Charlie would do for Christmas Day. Her yearning to be with them was silly, she knew. She hadn't remembered anything about *before*. She didn't like Christmas, she'd told him several times.

Still, she would have felt better not being alone.

The Ridgeville Inn very kindly gave them three rooms on the same floor—two connecting ones for the girls, and a room across the hall for Jayne. The girls all took turns flipping lights on and off, celebrating the luxury of life without flashlights. They switched on the televisions and immediately began to squabble over which program to watch. Jayne had to referee the fight over renting "in room" films, as well.

"One movie a day in one room a day," she told them.

"But I haven't seen any of these movies," Taryn wailed. "Can't we have a movie in each room? Every day?"

"No."

"Could we have two movies a day in one room?"

"No. One movie, one room, each day. And no adult ratings. General audience movies only."

Monique groaned. "We might as well watch cartoons."

"Those are the rules. If I discover you've broken them—and I will, because I'll have daily printouts of the room charges—there will be consequences, just as if we were still in school."

"Can we have room service?" Beth asked. "They have chips and dips, and cheese trays and hot artichoke dip with pita toast and—"

"That's the good news." She smiled at them. "The pizza restaurant is closed for the holiday." Predictable groans greeted her announcement. "Room service is our best option. So you can study the menu and decide what you'd like to eat while I take a shower." She turned to Sarah. "Don't let them loose."

Sarah smiled. "We'll be fine."

The problem with being alone was that she had too much time to think…about Chris. She pictured him driving down the mountain, turning onto River Road and pulling to a stop at his grandfather's house. Her mind showed her a wood cabin with a stone chimney—was that memory, or something he'd told her?

He'd mentioned the cabin in the stories, she recalled, when Juliet—she—had visited. Today, Charlie, his grandfather, would be glad to see him. Chris would get into clean clothes—his old ones had been a little rank—and the two men, old and young, would talk. Maybe Chris would tell him about finding Juliet. And losing her again.

Out of the shower, Jayne took the time to rub lotion on every inch of skin she could reach. The steamy mirror reflected a blurred image of her body—not the slim, agile form of a girl who could climb mountains and trees and do somersaults through the grass. Jayne didn't remember ever being slender. Had Elizabeth Jayne fattened her up as a disguise, like a goose being raised to provide liver for paté?

Such treachery still stunned her. She turned the blow dryer on High, hoping to blow out or brush off the hurt. It didn't work, of course, but clean lingerie, slacks, shirt and sweater left her feeling ready for almost anything. Even room service for eight.

She allowed the girls to order anything they wanted, which turned out better than she expected. Yes, the servers delivered seven different appetizer dishes, and five different large pizzas blanketed an entire bed. But at the end of the evening, only three boxes of leftovers remained. Jayne suspected those would be empty before long.

"No one leaves this floor until tomorrow morning," she told them, giving her instructions for the night. "No one leaves their room after eleven, so get the drinks and candy bars you want before then. Be quiet in the hallway—other people are trying to sleep. We don't have anywhere else to go if they kick us out. Except back to Hawkridge."

"Oh, we wouldn't want to go there," Yolanda declared.

"No movies," Haley added.

"Exactly," Jayne said, smiling. "Do not destroy the room, the furniture or the televisions. Please avoid spilling drinks and grinding food into the carpet. Remember, one movie in one room."

"Shoot," Taryn muttered. "I hoped you'd forget."

Selena looked at her with eyebrows raised. "This is Tommy you're talking about."

"Ahem." Jayne cleared her throat. "I expect you to represent the school in a way that makes me proud. If you need anything, don't hesitate to call. Just dial my room number, 593. Questions?"

The girls shook their heads.

"Then I hope you have a good night watching free TV and one movie rated for general audiences."

"We got the message," Beth said, holding the door for her to leave. "Good night, Ms. Thomas."

"Good night, girls."

Smiling, Jayne crossed the hall and let herself into her own room. She'd never gotten to know a group of students quite so well. She would miss them when school started and life returned to normal.

Just as she pulled her pajama top over her head, the phone rang.

Maybe she wouldn't miss them, after all. How could they possibly need her again already?

She sighed and picked up the phone. "What now?"

Chris said, "I guess you were expecting someone else?"

HE HEARD HER GASP over the phone line. "I, um, I thought the girls were calling."

Always the girls. He supposed he'd better get used to it. "Do you need to keep the line free? I can let you go."

"Oh, no. That's… I mean, they can come across the hall, if it's an emergency."

"You have a room to yourself? That's a restful change." And this was a silly conversation, not at all what he wanted to say.

"I'm not sure the girls won't jump out of their rooms like

popcorn kernels escaping a hot kettle." She gave that low chuckle he loved. "But the absence of noise is wonderful."

"I'm glad. You deserve…well, a lot of wonderful things." Could he sound more adolescent? "I wanted to wish you a Merry Christmas."

"Oh." After a pause, she said, "Merry Christmas to you, Chris." Her voice sounded…warm. Almost happy. "Did you get to your grandfather's house without trouble?"

"Not exactly."

"What happened?"

"Charlie's sick." He described his panicked exit from the doctor's office to the hospital.

"Oh, Chris, I'm so sorry. Will he recover?"

"This time, probably. He's on his third round with the cancer, though, and the chemo is just to keep him as comfortable as possible." He wiped his eyes on the sleeve of his T-shirt. "They aren't sure how long he'll last."

"I know that must be hard for you. Watching someone you love fade away requires more strength than seems possible, sometimes." Her soft tone and gentle words gave him comfort he hadn't known he needed.

He hoped he had the strength to offer the same. "You were with your grandmother when she passed away, weren't you?"

"Yes. Except…" The gentleness disintegrated, to be replaced with cold steel.

Chris hardened his own resolve. "She wasn't really your grandmother, you were going to say?"

"Well, evidently she wasn't. There's…proof."

"I've been thinking about Elizabeth Jayne." He cleared his throat. "Although it's easy to be angry about what she did, maybe we have to offer her some understanding."

"I don't see how that's possible."

"Suppose the family she told you about was real—she lost her grandkids plus her daughter and son-in-law in a fire. That's a huge blow for a woman alone."

"Yes."

"So one night, she comes across a young girl wandering on the mountain. This girl has no ID on her and can't say who she is or where she's from."

"The responsible, moral, reasonable thing to do is take the girl to a hospital and let the police find out where she belongs."

"True. But this woman has suffered a grievous loss, and maybe she's not quite sane." Chris kept his voice even, despite the tension on both ends of the line. "Or maybe she never was quite sane, which is why she lived alone on a mountain. Anyway, this girl has mahogany curls, like her daughter and granddaughter had. She doesn't remember anything about herself, and she's terrified.

"The old woman takes to calling the girl Jayne, which was her mother's and her daughter's name. Soon enough the girl *is* Jayne to her. They have a relationship."

"Built on lies." Her brittle tone eased a fraction.

"Actually, I think the foundation was kindness—the old woman took care of this girl when she was hurt. Remember that Good Samaritan story I mentioned before?"

The dam broke suddenly. Jayne's "yes" was buried in the midst of sniffs and smothered sobs.

"It was pretty easy, I imagine, to fill in the memories with her own—memories of her daughter's childhood and what she knew of her granddaughter's. Maybe…maybe Elizabeth Jayne rebuilt her life around the girl she found on the mountain."

After a minute, his Jayne whispered thickly, "Hold on. I'll

be back." In the distance, he could hear her blowing her nose, which made him smile.

Then she said, "I'm here," into the phone. "Thank you."

"We can probably check some of this out," he told her. "The family, the fire…there will be records. If you want to know."

She sighed. "Perhaps. One day."

That seemed to be enough drama for tonight. "Charlie would like you to visit him," Chris said then, more briskly. "If you don't mind."

"I'll be glad to visit, as long as you don't mind keeping watch over seven rambunctious girls."

"I can do that." They settled the details for meeting the next morning. Then they both yawned at the same time.

"Did you turn up the heat in your room?" he asked.

Jayne chuckled. "It's set on seventy-four. Is the cabin warm?"

"I'm at the inn, too. And I've got the thermostat set at seventy-six." His room was directly below hers, as a matter of fact, which was a kind of torture all by itself. He could go to her…the girls would never know. They could be alone…

Then she yawned again, hugely, audibly. And sniffed. "I'm sorry."

"It's okay. You've had a long week. Sleep well, Ms. Thomas. I'll see you and the girls at the hospital tomorrow morning."

"You, too, Chris."

He put the phone down before she did, turned off the bedside light and crawled between the sheets, which could have been burlap, for all he noticed at that point.

They knew most of the facts now, but he wasn't sure truth had simplified the situation. If he'd met Jayne without recognizing her and they'd fallen in love in the usual way, Chris didn't think there would be a problem.

Instead, he'd been a stupid jerk and barged into her life at exactly the wrong time, told her the sad old story in the worst possible way and demanded she remember being the girl who loved him. How could Jayne know what she felt for him now?

Worse, why should she believe him when he said he loved her? As a boy, he'd adored Juliet with all the conviction in his young heart. But did anyone love at thirty the way they loved at fifteen?

His feelings for Jayne Thomas would always be different, because *he* was different. He loved Jayne as a man loves his woman, with the passion and endurance of an adult, for better or worse, richer or poorer, in sickness and in health. Without the same kind of love on her side, how could they build a solid life together?

Half a loaf, they said—whoever "they" might be—was better than none.

Chris very much doubted that the same could be said of love.

THE SMALL RIDGEVILLE HOSPITAL stood only a few blocks off Main Street. After a late breakfast, Jayne prodded the girls into their jackets and started them on the short walk from the inn. The snow had largely melted off the roads and sidewalks, and the temperature had climbed into the forties.

"It feels like summertime," Beth declared, pulling off her hat. "I'm getting hot in this coat."

Haley squinted down the street. "The bank sign says forty-two degrees." She had an appointment with a doctor that afternoon to have her wrist examined, but the bruising and swelling had decreased quite a bit in the last two days.

"The snowmen are melting," Sarah pointed out as they walked past the houses on Fledgling Street. "It's so sad."

Jayne kept her eyes and half her attention on the girls, but looked ahead as well, wanting a glimpse of Chris as soon as possible. She'd hugged him less than twenty-four hours ago, and they'd talked within the last twelve. But she wanted to see him.

She was searching so hard, in the end she missed him entirely. Her gaze passed over the tall, lean figure in an Irish knit sweater and gray corduroy jeans as she sought a heavier figure in a worn, too-big parka and dirty denims.

So the girls saw him first. "Mr. Hammond!" they screamed, practically in unison, and went running down the sidewalk. Jayne, blushing and with her heart pounding, followed.

At least she arrived after the hugs had been accomplished, and didn't have to try to endure such casual contact.

"There you are," she said, sounding only a little breathless. She hoped.

"Good morning. Did you sleep like a rock?" He gave her his smile, and she studied his smooth face, his clean, wavy hair blowing in the slight breeze and the sharp blue brilliance of his eyes. Lord, the man was handsome.

What had he asked? "Oh…oh, yes. Definitely. Did you have enough room to stretch out?" They fell in step together as the girls explored the residual snow on the lawn of the hospital.

"I woke up lying on my back, with a hand or a foot in each corner."

Jayne stopped in her tracks and gazed at him. "I don't believe you."

Chris chuckled. "Not really. But I had a good night's rest." They reached the entrance and stopped again. Hands in his pockets, he said, "Charlie's in room 258. He's excited that you're coming."

"I'm glad to be here," she stated honestly.

"And don't worry about the girls. I'll keep them out of trouble."

Thinking back to the week before, when she'd feared he might be an ax murderer or a pedophile, as well as her personal stalker, Jayne smiled. "I know you will. I trust you." She walked into the hospital without a backward glance.

On the second floor, she located Charlie's room and peeked around the door, in case he was resting.

But the man in the bed immediately held out a hand. "Come on in. Let me see you."

Jayne crossed the room and, when he kept his hand out, felt she had no choice but to take it. "I'm Jayne Thomas, Mr. Hammond."

"Call me Charlie. I know who you are. And who you were." He stared at her, his brows drawn together. Despite the gray hair and the ravages of age, she could see Chris in his face.

"I can tell why he recognized you," Charlie concluded. "You're plumper, all grown up and filled out. But there's something of Juliet in your eyes. And in that mouth of yours. Have a seat."

Blinking at the notion of being "plumper" and "filled out," Jayne sat. "I'm sorry you're not well."

He waved the comment away with the same gesture Chris used. "I'm seventy-eight. Folks die. Christopher says you don't remember him, or those times. Do you want to?"

"I…"

Charlie didn't break the silence as Jayne considered whether she did, indeed, want to remember her life as Juliet.

"No, I don't think I do." She said it with a shiver of surprise. "There seems to have been a lot of pain involved. I don't think I—Juliet—was ever very happy. Except here in the mountains, with you and Chris."

"I'd say that was true. Even here, though, the two of you

always had the next separation hanging over you. It's hard to think straight when you know you have to say goodbye soon."

"It is."

She'd been gazing at their clasped hands. When Charlie didn't saying anything for a little too long, she looked up, worried, only to find he'd dozed off. Would he sleep a long time? Should she leave?

Before she'd decided, his eyes snapped open again. "For what it's worth, Christopher has done some changing these last few days. He's not the same boy who left my house and rode off into a blizzard."

"That's funny," Jayne replied. "Because I think I am the same woman he fell on top of at the front door of the school that night. More or less, anyway."

Charlie nodded. "Good. Things'll work out just right, if that's the case. He needed a woman, not the selfish young girl he's mourned all these years." He took a sip of water, coughed and then squeezed her hand. "Now, tell me where you went to school. What kind of courses did you take?"

They talked about education and the beauty of the Smoky Mountains and her junior year in Spain, where he'd also spent some time, until Charlie began to look tired.

"I'm going," Jayne told him, standing by the bed. "But I'll see you again soon."

"You will." He closed his eyes as she bent to kiss his cheek. "Count on it. And tell Christopher to keep the heat on in my house, 'cause I'm going home at the end of this week, whether that damn doctor likes it or not!"

Chapter Fourteen

Chris treated them all to pizza for lunch. While he spent the evening at the hospital with his grandfather, Ms. Thomas subjected her students to an etiquette lesson in the inn's formal dining room, complete with soupspoons, ice-cream forks and different glasses for each type of wine—filled with soda, of course.

On the following morning, the comforts of the twenty-first century, including electricity, returned to Hawkridge Manor. Once the maintenance company for the generator rushed out to repair it at no cost, and apologized profusely for a faulty switch, Jayne took her girls back to their school. The close quarters at the hotel had them all getting on each other's nerves. And hers.

Jayne had called all the parents from the hotel that first night to assure them their daughters were safe and in a suitable environment. Now she called again to report the move back to home ground. Though Monique's parents and Taryn's grandparents had intended to bring them home for the holiday, both girls asked to stay at school until classes started again in January. The relief in their families' voices was painfully easy to hear.

So they settled back into their routine—minus cooking on

the fire. They were all grateful for hot food and drinks at the turn of a knob.

But when Jayne suggested, the first night back, that the girls could go to their own beds, Haley was the first to protest. "Can't we sleep down here?"

Beth nodded. "Sleeping by the fire was cool."

"It was warm," Monique corrected. She winked at Beth. "But I liked it, too. It's only a few more days."

"We've still got our blanket rolls made up," Sarah added in a hopeful voice.

"Those need to be washed," Jayne announced. Then she grinned. "But it can wait until tomorrow."

The manor sat higher on the mountain than Ridgeville, and the temperatures hadn't climbed enough to completely melt the huge quantity of snow. The girls had spent their afternoon outside and were, as a result, quite tired after dinner. Taryn and Haley fell asleep before the movie on the television was halfway over. Jayne sat under a lamp in the far corner, knitting with the mohair yarn she'd purchased on that first morning, when Chris had been stalking her. She smiled at the memory.

"Ms. Thomas?" Serena stood in front of her. "The movie's over. Would it be okay if we turned off the TV?"

Jayne tried to hide her shock. "Of course. What are you going to do instead?"

The girl shrugged. "Talk a little, I guess. Just be quiet. It's nice to listen to the crackle of the fire."

What a change from the usual dependence on mass-produced sources of entertainment. Jayne didn't expect the transformation to be permanent. They would return to average teenage habits soon enough. But perhaps, when they became adults, they would remember this week of self-sufficiency and bring it back into their lives.

Thanks, in no small part, to Chris.

Jayne let her knitting fall into her lap, leaned her head against the wing of the chair and closed her eyes. She didn't know what to expect from him now. Would he see that Charlie was taken care of and then go back to his job, somewhere halfway around the world? That had been his intention, she was sure. His grandfather said he'd changed during the last week. But that could be just wishful thinking on the part of a fond old man.

As to her own future…nothing would change there unless she chose. Hawkridge would be here and would continue to need a headmistress. She liked the job and was good at it. What else did she need to know?

An image flashed in front of her closed eyes—of a snowy night, a winding road, an open convertible. Maybe her imagination had supplied the details…or was it her memory? She could see the red upholstery in the car, smell wax and leather and the scent of pines in the air. He'd been wearing a leather jacket with a sheepskin lining, but no gloves. His fingers were icy cold when he reached for her face, forcing her to look at him.

Hot tears and cold snowflakes touched her cheeks at the same moment.

The phone rang on the table beside her. Shocked by the unfamiliar noise, Jayne jerked upright, which sent her knitting sliding to the floor. She picked up the receiver first, then bent to retrieve her needles. "The Hawkridge School," she said, panting. "Headmistress Jayne Thomas speaking."

"I'm glad to hear that," Chris told her with a grin in his voice. "I'd have been worried if anybody else answered."

Jayne told herself it was the bending over that left her breathless. "Where are you?"

"Charlie's. Are you okay?"

"Of course." She drew a deep breath in through her nose, hoping to calm down. "How is Charlie?"

"Good. They're going to release him on Friday."

"That's wonderful to hear. He's feeling better?"

"According to Charlie, he never felt bad in the first place."

She chuckled. "Of course." Then she sobered as the need to know his plans overcame her. "Do you, um, expect to stay with him for a while? Or do you have to rush off to some new crisis?"

"I don't have to rush."

That wasn't an answer, but she hesitated to push any harder. "I'm sure your granddad will enjoy the time you spend together."

"I expect he'll be as crabby as usual within an hour of stepping through his own front door. Which is what I wanted to talk to you about."

"Oh?" One word was all she could manage.

"I wondered if you and the girls would like to come over and welcome Charlie home."

He spoke as if this was the most reasonable idea in the world, as if they were lifelong friends. As if they were *family.*

Jayne didn't want to hope. "Won't seven teenagers be too much for Charlie when he's just out of the hospital?"

"He asked if you all could visit. He wants to meet the girls. And he'd like to see you again."

She wasn't sure she believed Chris, but how could she refuse? *Why* should she? One last day with him wouldn't hurt anyone. "Then we'd be glad to join you."

"Great." The word sounded like a sigh of relief. "I'll let you know exactly what time we'll be there."

A silence followed, which Jayne felt compelled to break. "I want to thank you again for all—"

"No way." On the other end of the line, Chris cursed himself for not saying it first. "The debt in this situation is all mine," he insisted. "You rescued me out of the storm, literally."

"You were so much help with the girls—"

"Then the honors are even and we need to forget about that." He didn't want gratitude from Jayne Thomas.

Another silence demanded to be filled. "Are the girls all wrapped in their separate earphones, listening to their own sounds?" He had to laugh when she told him they'd turned off the TV to sleep. "One small step for civilization," he suggested.

Then he realized she might want to get to bed, herself. "You've had a busy few days and you must be tired. I'll let you go to sleep," he offered, though the vision of Jayne in bed did not inspire him with the desire to snooze. "They'll be awake early tomorrow morning, I bet."

Her sweet chuckle rippled through him. "And they know where the microwave, the bagels and the instant oatmeal are. They're pretty self-reliant these days."

"Who would have thought?" This time, he distinctly heard Jayne yawn. "Get a good night's rest. I'll call again when I know more about Charlie's schedule." After a second, he added, "And even if I don't."

She hesitated, then said, "I would like that."

And Chris went to sleep with a smile on his face.

THE PLAN EVOLVED over three phone calls the next day and one last call early Friday morning. Lunch plans enlarged from sandwiches and chips to a roast turkey, started by Chris in the morning, and side dishes prepared by the girls to please every individual taste.

"We look like a catering company," Jayne commented as

they loaded boxes and bowls into the back of the school van at 8:00 a.m. "Maybe that could be a Hawkridge sideline."

"It's pretty hard work." Monique carried out a heavy bowl of potato salad. "I vote no."

Taryn groaned under the weight of a huge tossed salad. "I like cooking. But not this much."

Yolanda, however, was hooked. "I'm going to look at colleges with catering programs. This is so much fun, and I can't wait to taste my mama's sweet-potato casserole." She'd supplied the recipe from memory.

"Neither can I," Jayne assured her. "Now, do we have everything?" A quick survey revealed the absence of cranberry sauce.

"All of you get into the van," Jayne instructed. "I'll fetch the sauce."

As she started out of the kitchen, though, the telephone rang. She was tempted to ignore it, but if a parent called and didn't get an answer…

"Good morning." Chris's rough, early-morning voice responded to her standard greeting. "Are you awake?"

"I'll have you know we're loaded into the van and ready to drive. While you sound like you just rolled off the mattress."

"Not yet, actually. I've got half an hour before I have to leave."

"Oh, well, that's plenty of time."

"Do I hear sarcasm?"

"Oh, yes."

He sighed. "I thought so."

Jayne waited a moment, but he didn't say anything else. "Chris? Is something wrong?"

"No. I just…" She could picture him rubbing a hand over his face in the pause. "I had a rough night. I dreamed you left. And never came back."

She swallowed a flicker of anger, a spark of hurt. "We call that *déjà vu*."

"No, no, not Juliet. You. Jayne Thomas."

Now she had to swallow back tears. "Well, my only travel plans at the moment involve getting a van loaded with seven girls and a lot of delicious food to Charlie's cabin in the next hour."

She heard him draw a breath, then loudly exhale. "I can live with that. See you about noon?"

"Definitely."

"Good."

"I'LL MAKE YOU A DEAL," Chris told his granddad as they waited for the wheelchair to arrive.

"What?" Charlie paced to the window. "I can walk out," he grumbled. "Why do they always make me take the damn chair?"

"So you don't fall. So you don't sue them because you fell."

"I wouldn't do that."

"That's what they all say. Do you want to hear the deal?"

"Sure. What's the deal?"

"If you don't complain from here to the car about the wheelchair, I'll let you walk by yourself into your own house."

Charlie stared at him with narrowed eyes. "There's another option?"

Chris stood up from the bed. "Sure. You've lost enough weight, I don't think I'd have any trouble throwing you over my shoulder and carrying you in."

His granddad straightened up. "You think you could?"

Stepping closer, Chris looked down at the older man. "I know I could."

Rolling his eyes, Charlie looked away. "I'll complain if I want to."

But he kept every thought to himself as the nursing aide

pushed his chair down the hall and into the elevator, then out to the front entrance of the hospital where the Hawkridge sedan waited.

"You're driving the school car?" Charlie lowered himself into the passenger seat. "What's that about?"

"Jayne let me borrow it. Your piece of junk is still parked at the doctor's office." Chris shut the door and went around to the driver's side.

Charlie started to bristle. "That car is…" The words trailed off and he sighed. "A piece of junk. I just don't see the point of buying a new one."

Chris ignored the implication. "Don't worry about it. I can drive you around while I'm here."

"Last I heard, you were planning to leave New Year's Day."

"Plans change." He tipped the visor down against the bright winter sunshine.

"Do they?"

Chris took a deep breath. "Maybe."

With a satisfied "Ah," Charlie relaxed against the seat. "I hope you've got something good planned for lunch."

The drive to Charlie's place took an easy fifteen minutes. Chris grinned when he saw fresh tire tracks in the soft mud of the drive. Jayne and the girls had arrived.

In fact, the girls came pouring out onto the front porch as soon as he braked the car. Charlie looked at the group and then at Chris. "We have company for lunch?"

"Yep."

"Good. And we made a deal, right?"

"We did."

With a decisive nod, Charlie pushed the car door open and hauled himself up out of the seat.

"Don't forget it," he told Chris. Then he walked on his

own, head high, back straight and steps firm, to greet his guests on the porch.

Chris didn't get a chance to talk to Jayne until all of them had settled into chairs around his granddad's farm table. He leaned to his right, where she sat beside him. "The food looks terrific."

She nodded, keeping an eye out as the dishes were passed around. "You did a great job with the turkey. It was perfectly done when we got here."

He helped himself to sweet potatoes and passed the bowl to Jayne. "I just followed your instructions."

"That's a skill I appreciate." She picked up her fork and took a quick bite of the potatoes while he was still ladling dressing onto his plate. "Mmm. Yolanda's mother has a fabulous recipe. Is Charlie feeling okay?"

"Physically, who knows? Mentally, he's as sharp as ever. He was pleased to see all the girls here. And you."

"It's a very special day."

Chris barely stopped himself from saying, "I hope so." He appreciated the effort the girls and Jayne had taken to create this dinner, but he couldn't bring himself to eat, wouldn't be able to until he was sure…sure of Jayne, sure of their future together. The only way to be sure was to talk to her. Alone.

Yet here they were, in a small cabin with eight other people. That was why he'd cornered Sarah as soon as he got into the house—to get this right, he needed help.

After finishing up a second piece of pecan pie, Charlie slapped his hands on the table. "That was a meal worth coming home for." He nodded his head at Jayne. "My compliments to you and your cooks, Ms. Thomas. All I need now is a cigar and a glass of brandy and the day will be perfect."

"No cigar," Chris told him. "You know that. And it's a little early in the day for brandy. Maybe tonight."

Charlie started to protest, but Jayne spoke first. "We'll get the kitchen cleaned up." She scooted her chair back and stood. "The girls would like to explore a bit, and then we'll be heading back to the school."

"Ms. Thomas?" Just as Chris started to panic, Sarah leaned forward from her chair at the other end of the table. "We can take care of cleanup, especially if Uncle Charlie tells us where to put things." She glanced at him and smiled, which drove the old man's scowl right off his face. "Just leave it to us."

Around the table, the girls nodded their heads as Jayne looked from one to the other.

"Okay," she said, and Chris could breathe again. "I'll investigate the fascinating books on the shelves, instead."

"Or—" Chris stepped close enough to lower his voice "—we could go for a walk."

She lifted one eyebrow as she gazed at him. "Am I the victim of a plot?"

"Yes."

"I'll get my coat."

The clear blue skies of noontime had given way to silver-edged clouds driven by a blustery wind. Both of them buttoned their coats up before stepping off the porch.

"I'm sure this place is beautiful in the spring." Jayne brushed her hand across the low branch of a dogwood tree. "Are there daffodils everywhere?"

"Used to be." Chris captured that free hand with one of his own. "I doubt he's dug them up."

Her fingers nestled warmly between his. "I'd love to see it."

They rounded the corner of the house and got their first glimpse of the pond out back. The surrounding forest shaded a long, steep hill sloping down from the cabin, which kept snow on their sledding run for most of the winter. Rimmed by willow trees and hardwoods, the pond's silver water reflected a stormy sky.

Jayne halted briefly. "How lovely." She kept her gaze on the view as they walked to the lip of the hill, where she again stood motionless.

Chris waited in the silence. He didn't want to push her, didn't want to speak too soon.

Finally, a huge sigh lifted her shoulders. She turned to him, her eyes dark with tears. "I don't remember." Tears choked her voice, too. "I don't remember any of this." She bent her head until her forehead rested against his chest. "I should at least remember Charlie."

"There's no 'should' to this situation." Chris used his free hand to cradle the nape of her neck. "It is the way it is."

She sobbed, once, and proceed to cry quietly as he held her against him.

When she eventually drew back, he handed her the handkerchief he'd jammed in his pocket for just this purpose.

"Thank you," she said, after clearing her throat. Then she looked up, directly into his face. "What if I never remember?"

He shrugged one shoulder. "I don't think it matters, Jayne. That's the past. We don't live there anymore."

Her expression remained doubtful. "What if you can't forget?"

"Then I'll be like everybody else, with a girlfriend in my past and a beautiful, vibrant woman to love in the present."

"You make it sound easy."

"I know damn well it's not easy for you." He couldn't help the harshness in his voice. "I came into your life badgering you and ordering you around and, oh, yeah, falling on top of you and dragging you to the floor."

Jayne pretended to rub a bruise on her shoulder. "I remember that."

"The first time I kissed you, and the second, I was trying to force you to remember something—to be someone I wanted. Something I thought I needed."

"Yes. I slapped you for it, too."

"Not hard or often enough." He grinned slightly. "I deserved to be kicked in the butt and thrown out in the snow. But you...you took me in, made me warm. Kept me alive."

He pulled her close again. "Your kisses weren't like anything I'd ever known. I didn't even realize what I needed in my life until I kissed you, Jayne Thomas. Until I held you, and you held me."

His frown didn't lighten, and she turned her hands so she could grip his in return. "What's wrong, Chris? What are you trying to say?"

He shook his head, staring at their hands. "I want to be good to you, Jayne. You probably can't believe I have that in me, but I do. I can be kind, and honest, and patient. Not all the time, I guess. But I don't usually treat women like...like hostages. And I'll never be cruel to you again. I swear."

She gave his hands a shake. "What makes you think you need to tell me this?"

"I know how I behaved."

"I know what I saw, Christopher Hammond. I saw your kindness, when you put yourself out to distract a bunch of spoiled brats whining because they couldn't watch television.

"I saw your sense of fun and fair play, when you let them win snowball fights, when you carried their sleds for them up the hills, when you gave them a Peace Tree and spent the day patiently making their visions come to life.

"Your honesty was always on display, of course." She

winked at him. "You never hesitated to let me know what you thought."

Finally, his lovely mouth curved into a smile.

"You're a good man. I knew that early on, if not right away. And…" She needed a deep breath to finish. "And I love you."

He brought her hands to his lips, keeping his gaze on hers. "Does that mean you'll marry me, Jayne Thomas?"

"I can't remember a time when I wanted anything else."

Chris dipped his head and Jayne put her arms around his neck, drawing him down for a kiss.

If they heard the applause and cheers coming from inside the cabin, they chose not to notice.

ABANDONING HIS PLANE reservation and his next assignment, Chris stayed on with Charlie, sorting through the books and clothes and papers of a lifetime. Without needing to say a word on the subject, he and Jayne scheduled their wedding as soon as possible after school started again in the New Year. Just to be safe.

That was how Chris found himself, on a Saturday afternoon during a warm spell referred to as "blackberry winter," standing at the front of the dining hall at Hawkridge. Charlie stood beside him, both of them wearing what his granddad called "monkey suits," and waiting for the music to start.

Facing him were all of Jayne's students, plus the entire school staff—including Mr. Trevino, wearing the new winter coat Chris had given him.

"Don't drop the ring," Charlie whispered.

"I don't have the ring," Chris said quietly, for the third time. "You have the ring."

"I do?" Charlie patted his pockets. "Now, where would it be, I wonder?"

"I am not going to panic," Chris told him. "If you lose the ring, no problem. I'm not nervous. This is the best thing that's ever happened to me in my life." He winked at his granddad. "Besides growing up with you."

Charlie gave a snort. "You're no fun."

The Hawkridge String Ensemble began to play at that moment, and the doors to the dining hall opened from the outside. Taryn and Haley came down the center aisle between the rows of chairs, wearing dark red dresses and looking almost too excited to breathe. Beth and Selena followed, dressed in dark green gowns, pretending to be too old for nerves. Yolanda and Monique, in midnight-blue, lived up to their promise as young women facing the future with strength and grace. Sarah walked in by herself, as the maid of honor. She wore a vivid teal dress and carried the same white lilies in her bouquet as the others.

Chris turned to the girls and gave them what he hoped was a decent bow. "Seven has always been my lucky number," he said. "You all look beautiful."

The music changed, and he looked up just as Jayne stepped through the doorway. She started toward him, holding the arm of her friend Mason Reed, a former teacher at the school.

Good thing this is our wedding, Chris thought. *Otherwise, I'd be jealous. The guy is too damn handsome.*

He couldn't stop grinning as she walked toward him, wearing the smile he loved and her hair curling around her shoulders. The cream dress she'd chosen was nice, though she could have shaved her head or worn biker leather and he'd be just as happy.

She was here. Nothing else mattered.

"Hello, stranger," she said as she stepped up beside him in front of the minister. "Don't I remember you from somewhere?"

He leaned close enough to whisper, "I'm the guy who's taking you to paradise tonight."

Her smile deepened. "I'll hold you to that."

Chris thought he heard a chuckle from Mason Reed on her other side.

Charlie hadn't lost the ring, of course, though his fingers trembled as he reached into his breast pocket at that point in the service.

"Be happy, both of you," he said, clasping Jayne's hand with his free one as he offered the golden circle to Chris. Then he stepped back, pulled out his handkerchief and wiped tears from his cheeks.

Chris turned back to Jayne and locked his gaze with hers. "I, Christopher, take you, Jayne," he said, without prompting, "to be my lawfully wedded wife. To have and to hold, from this day forward." He'd been waiting to say this for weeks. "For better or worse, for richer or poorer, in sickness and in health. Forsaking all others, as long as we both shall live." He slipped the band on her finger, and bent to kiss her hand.

Sarah handed his ring to Jayne, and she began the same promise. "I, Jayne, take you, Christopher, to be my lawfully wedded husband." The time-honored words went straight to his heart. He would keep them there forever.

They said the final words of the pledge together. "And thereto I plight thee my troth."

"Which means," Chris translated for the benefit of the bridesmaids, "I may now kiss my bride."

With seven tearful girls surrounding them, in front of three hundred swooning students, smiling faculty and his grandfather, that's exactly what he did.

* * * * *

*Celebrate 60 years of pure reading pleasure
with Harlequin®!
Just in time for the holidays,
Silhouette Special Edition® is proud to present
New York Times bestselling author
Kathleen Eagle's
ONE COWBOY, ONE CHRISTMAS*

Rodeo rider Zach Beaudry was a travelin' man—until he broke down in middle-of-nowhere South Dakota during a deep freeze. That's when an angel came to his rescue....

a hairdresser, and he was feeling...vig time, he
have given his right arm to be climbing into a hotel hot tu
instead of a brutal blast of north wind. The right was his fr

"Don't die on me. Come on, Zel. You know how much I love you, girl. You're all I've got. Don't do this to me here. Not *now*."

But Zelda had quit on him, and Zach Beaudry had no one to blame but himself. He'd taken his sweet time hitting the road, and then miscalculated a shortcut. For all he knew he was a hundred miles from gas. But even if they were sitting next to a pump, the ten dollars he had in his pocket wouldn't get him out of South Dakota, which was not where he wanted to be right now. Not even his beloved pickup truck, Zelda, could get him much of anywhere on fumes. He was sitting out in the cold in the middle of nowhere. And getting colder.

He shifted the pickup into Neutral and pulled hard on the steering wheel, using the downhill slope to get her off the blacktop and into the roadside grass, where she shuddered to a standstill. He stroked the padded dash. "You'll be safe here."

But Zach would not. It was getting dark, and it was already too damn cold for his cowboy ass. Zach's battered body was a barometer, and he was feeling South Dakota, big time. He'd have given his right arm to be climbing into a hotel hot tub instead of a brutal blast of north wind. The right was his free arm anyway. Damn thing had lost altitude, touched some part of the bull and caused him a scoreless ride last time out.

It wasn't scoring him a ride this night, either. A carload of teenagers whizzed by, topping off the insult by laying on the horn as they passed him. It was at least twenty minutes before another vehicle came along. He stepped out and waved both arms this time, damn near getting himself killed. Whatever happened to *do unto others?* In places like this, decent people didn't leave each other stranded in the cold.

His face was feeling stiff, and he figured he'd better start walking before his toes went numb. He struck out for a distant yard light, the only sign of human habitation in sight. He couldn't tell how distant, but he knew he'd be hurting by the time he got there, and he was counting on some kindly old man to be answering the door. No shame among the lame.

It wasn't like Zach was fresh off the operating table—it had been a few months since his last round of repairs—but he hadn't given himself enough time. He'd lopped a couple of weeks off the near end of the doc's estimated recovery time, rigged up a brace, done some heavy-duty taping and climbed onto another bull. Hung in there for five seconds—four seconds past feeling the pop in his hip and three seconds short of the buzzer.

He could still feel the pain shooting down his leg with every step. Only this time he had to pick the damn thing up, swing it forward and drop it down again on his own.

Pride be damned, he just hoped *somebody* would be answering the door at the end of the road. The light in the front window was a good sign.

The four steps to the covered porch might as well have been four hundred, and he was looking to climb them with a lead weight chained to his left leg. His eyes were just as screwed up as his hip. Big black spots danced around with tiny red flashers, and he couldn't tell what was real and what wasn't. He stumbled over some shrubbery, steadied himself on the porch railing and peered between vertical slats.

There in the front window stood a spruce tree with a silver star affixed to the top. Zach was pretty sure the red sparks were all in his head, but the white lights twinkling by the hundreds throughout the huge tree, those were real. He wasn't too sure about the woman hanging the shiny balls. Most of her hair was caught up on her head and fastened in a curly clump, but the light captured by the escaped bits crowned her with a golden halo. Her face was a soft shadow, her body a willowy silhouette beneath a long white gown. If this was where the mind ran off to when cold started shutting down the rest of the body, then Zach's final worldly thought was, *This ain't such a bad way to go.*

If she would just turn to the window, he could die looking into the eyes of a Christmas angel.

* * * * *

Could this woman from
Zach's past get the lonesome cowboy
to come in from the cold...for good?
Look for
ONE COWBOY, ONE CHRISTMAS
by Kathleen Eagle
Available December 2009 from
Silhouette Special Edition®

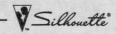

SPECIAL EDITION

**FROM *NEW YORK TIMES* AND *USA TODAY*
BESTSELLING AUTHOR**

KATHLEEN EAGLE

ONE COWBOY,
One Christmas

When bull rider Zach Beaudry appeared
out of thin air on Ann Drexler's ranch,
she thought she was seeing a ghost of
Christmas past. And though Zach had
no memory of their night of passion years
ago, they were about to share a future
he would never forget.

*Available December 2009
wherever books are sold.*

SSE65493

Visit Silhouette Books at www.eHarlequin.com

REQUEST YOUR FREE BOOKS!

2 FREE NOVELS PLUS 2 FREE GIFTS!

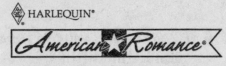

HARLEQUIN®

American Romance®

Love, Home & Happiness!

YES! Please send me 2 FREE Harlequin® American Romance® novels and my 2 FREE gifts (gifts are worth about $10). After receiving them, if I don't wish to receive any more books, I can return the shipping statement marked "cancel." If I don't cancel, I will receive 4 brand-new novels every month and be billed just $4.24 per book in the U.S. or $4.99 per book in Canada.* That's a savings of close to 15% off the cover price! It's quite a bargain! Shipping and handling is just 50¢ per book. I understand that accepting the 2 free books and gifts places me under no obligation to buy anything. I can always return a shipment and cancel at any time. Even if I never buy another book from Harlequin, the two free books and gifts are mine to keep forever.

154 HDN E4DS   354 HDN E4D4

Name	(PLEASE PRINT)

Address	Apt. #

City	State/Prov.	Zip/Postal Code

Signature (if under 18, a parent or guardian must sign)

Mail to the Harlequin Reader Service:
IN U.S.A.: P.O. Box 1867, Buffalo, NY 14240-1867
IN CANADA: P.O. Box 609, Fort Erie, Ontario L2A 5X3

Not valid to current subscribers of Harlequin® American Romance® books.

Want to try two free books from another line?
Call 1-800-873-8635 or visit www.morefreebooks.com.

* Terms and prices subject to change without notice. Prices do not include applicable taxes. N.Y. residents add applicable sales tax. Canadian residents will be charged applicable provincial taxes and GST. Offer not valid in Quebec. This offer is limited to one order per household. All orders subject to approval. Credit or debit balances in a customer's account(s) may be offset by any other outstanding balance owed by or to the customer. Please allow 4 to 6 weeks for delivery. Offer available while quantities last.

Your Privacy: Harlequin is committed to protecting your privacy. Our Privacy Policy is available online at www.eHarlequin.com or upon request from the Reader Service. From time to time we make our lists of customers available to reputable third parties who may have a product or service of interest to you. If you would prefer we not share your name and address, please check here. ☐

HAR09R2

HARLEQUIN
Ambassadors

Want to share your passion for reading Harlequin® Books?

Become a Harlequin Ambassador!

Harlequin Ambassadors are a group
of passionate and well-connected readers
who are willing to share their joy of reading
Harlequin® books with family and friends.

You'll be sent all the tools you need to spark
great conversation, including free books!

All we ask is that you share the romance
with your friends and family!

You'll also be invited to have a say in
new book ideas and exchange opinions
with women just like you!

To see if you qualify* to be a Harlequin Ambassador, please visit www.HarlequinAmbassadors.com.

*Please note that not everyone who applies to be a Harlequin Ambassador will
qualify. For more information please visit www.HarlequinAmbassadors.com.

Thank you for your participation.

BAP09BPA

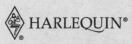

A Cowboy Christmas
MARIN THOMAS

2 stories in 1!

The holidays are a rough time for widower
Logan Taylor and single dad Fletcher McFadden—
neither hunky cowboy has been lucky in love.
But Christmas is the season of miracles! Logan
meets his match in "A Christmas Baby," while
Fletcher gets a second chance at love in "Marry
Me, Cowboy." This year both cowboys are on
Santa's Nice list!

***Available December
wherever books are sold.***

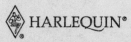

COMING NEXT MONTH
Available December 8, 2009

#1285 THE WRANGLER by Pamela Britton
Men Made in America

For as long as she can remember, Samantha Davies has dreamed of Montana's legendary Baer Mountain mustangs. She has to see for herself if there's truth behind the legend...before she loses her sight forever. And nothing, not even the devil-handsome wrangler Clint McAlister—who has every reason to distrust Samantha's intentions—is going to stand in her way. Because time is running out.

#1286 A MOMMY FOR CHRISTMAS by Cathy Gillen Thacker
The Lone Star Dads Club

With four preschoolers between them, neighbors and single parents Travis Carson and Holly Baxter don't know what they'd do without each other. And they don't want to find out! Everything changes when Travis's little girls ask Santa for a mommy for Christmas. Their entire Texas town gets in on the hunt for an available mom...who happens to live right next door.

#1287 HER CHRISTMAS WISH by Cindi Myers
The only thing Alina Allinova wants for Christmas is to stay in the U.S.—oh, and Eric Sepulveda. They're having a fairy-tale romance, yet the possibility of sharing a happily-ever-after seems far away, with her visa expiring soon. Still, her fingers are crossed that come Christmas morning she'll get her wish and find him under her tree!

#1288 A COWBOY CHRISTMAS by Marin Thomas
2 stories in 1!

The holidays are a rough time for widower Logan Taylor and single dad Fletcher McFadden—neither hunky cowboy has been lucky in love. But Christmas *is* the season of miracles! Logan meets his match in "A Christmas Baby," while Fletcher gets a second chance at love in "Marry Me, Cowboy." This year both cowboys are on Santa's Nice list!

www.eHarlequin.com

HARCNMBPA1109